Vanessa Robinson

Her Blood

Her Blood

Vanessa Robinson

Her Blood

A novel written by Vanessa Robinson

Published by Pages Turning

Her Blood

Her Blood published by Pages Turning LLC, Atlanta, GA

Cover by: Vanessa Robinson

A novel written by Vanessa Robinson

ISBN: 978-0-578-56375-6

Volume 1

Pages Turning Publishing LLC

Printed in the United States

/

Vanessa Robinson

Dedicated to the sisters in the universe who choose to walk their path following their dreams

Her Blood

Vanessa Robinson

Author Acknowledgements

Thank you to the Universe that allowed me the time and energy to complete this book. I stayed away from writing for a while but the characters just wouldn't shut up, so I had to bring this story to life.! It's been a long time coming! Thank you to all my supporters and loved ones. Lastly to the Most High, thank you for blessing me.

Her Blood

Vanessa Robinson

"Is solace anywhere more comforting than in the arms of a sister.
"

- Alice Walker

Her Blood

Vanessa Robinson

Her Blood

A novel written by Vanessa Robinson

Published by Pages Turning

Her Blood

Vanessa Robinson

Introduction

Tori relocated from Boston at thirty-one years old, to California with dreams of becoming a screen play writer. Tori thought she would finally find herself and begin the search for her blood family. She had set intentions on creating a life she was comfortable living, building wealth, but things were begging to fall apart at the seams. Tori imagined her career would be flourishing by now, life in California didn't quite turn out to be the dream she had for herself. Here it was three years after moving and the success was dwindling and the loneliness was roaring inside of her. Tori worked part-time as a receptionist at a writing agency booking freelance writers. The company was going bankrupt and so was she. Tori lived her life on her own, she was told she didn't have any living blood family, which she longed for her entire life. Living in California Tori had her good friend Mae, who she spent most of her time off work with. She often missed her friends back home and the change of seasons from fall to summer. Her favorite season was Autumn, strolling through the orange and red leaves, the bitter wind kissing her skin. It was spring time now and If she didn't make it career wise by the end of the year she was moving somewhere and starting over. That gave her six months to get it together. If she did make it, she would work on her career and finish the business she started with her good friend Will. William Richardson and Tori grew up together, he became the closest thing to family Tori had.

Will and Tori were the same age and went to the same schools together up until college when they started dating. Will owned and operated a dealership of luxury cars in Boston. In the financial strain she was going through, she knew she could call on him but refrained from doing so. Tori didn't want him to know she was having a hard time paying her mortgage, it was embarrassing to her. She moved thousands of miles away from home just to end up in the same struggle. Will was there for her when she was growing up and eventually became like a brother to her. Tori was given up for adoption at the age of three years old and raised by her foster mother Judy. Tori's foster mother was an angry woman who had no intentions of being nurturing and kind when she adopted her. Judy used the checks from the Department of Children Services to gamble and buy liquor. Judy would beat Tori when she drank. Judy drank so much liquor she would pass out with lit cigarettes on the couch nearby almost setting the house on fire. She would make Tori sleep on the floor when she didn't do something that pleased her. If her shoes weren't tied right or clean her room to her liking her foster mother would slap her repeatedly until her face was welted up. As a little girl, at five years old Tori had a magnanimous mind, and always forgiving, she was just wanted to be loved. Her hair hung long and curly and she had just a few freckles on her nose. Judy would tell her she was ugly and her parents didn't want her because they couldn't look at her disgusting face. Tori had three small dark red birthmarks on the left side of her face right below her ear. The birthmarks reminded her of the Hawaiian Islands clustered together. Judy knew the truth why Tori was given up for adoption and would never say who her real mother and father were. That woman dangled the information over her head like torture. Judy teased and manipulated her unmercifully. Judy would bend down low to Tori's face, the pungent smell of alcohol galvanizing her back in fear, but she could never get far back enough to avoid the smell. "Lil girl if you clean the whole house, I will tell you who your funky mammy and daddy are. If you clean up good when you're done, we can go see them." Tori would run off pig tails swinging, doing her best scrubbing every room spotless. When she was finished Judy would laugh at her and say, "This house is still nasty just like your fucking mother" flicking her cigarette on the freshly mopped floor and walk away. Tori would sit in her closet heartbroken crying into her pillow so Judy couldn't hear. After a while Tori stopped believing Judy would ever tell her who or where her family was, she wanted to run away from Judy house. After her first time trying to leave at Judy kept her bedroom door locked on the outside at night. Tori kept a picture of her birth mother given to her by a social worker during a visit when she was eight years old. The woman in the picture was young looking, caramel colored skin with dark eyes and long sandy brown hair. Her mother reminded her of the singer Phyllis Hyman, she was elegant with her diamond earrings and long lashes. Through the photo, her mother looked like she glided across the floor when she walked. Her mother's eyes were inviting and warm. Tori knew she had gotten her birthmarks and freckles from her birth mother. As a child she would often stare at the picture as a child and it would fill her up. When Judy starved her days for punishment, she would imagine her mother making her a stack of pancakes and eating together at the kitchen table laughing over spilled orange juice. Little Tori obsessed about finding her blood family, implanting in her mind if she could just find her family, she would be so happy. Tori was a naïve child who just wanted to be loved.

In school, none her classmates spoke to her and when they did it was always bullying. They refused to sit next to her because she smelled musty and her clothes were never clean. Judy only bought her three uniforms for school and barely bothered with the laundry. Tori had no choice to wear them over and over. The kids would walk past her in the hallways with their hands up to their noses as she walked by. In the classroom they threw balled up notebook paper at her as if she was trash. Tori often found mean notes pasted onto her locker saying "take a bath."

There was one chocolate skinned brown boy in the classroom who always found his way to sit next her. He would always sit down and smile at her but he never spoke. When the other kids snickered, he ignored them as if nothing happened. One day in art class, a tall girl who always had it out for Tori poured red paint on top of her head shouting "Look Tori's on her period!". As the red paint dripped down her face, staining her brown skin Tori sat frozen, unable to move and the tears began to pour out of her eyes. Then there he was, the boy who always smiled, wiping the paint off her face. He helped Tori up, grabbed her back pack and scolded the girl for what she had done. The boy grabbed Tori's hand and they snuck out of school. As they walked, they came to a stop in front of a white house trimmed with blue. It looked like a home from the magazines with a garden of flowers in the front yard. The boy finally broke his silence, with a bright smile washing over his face "I'm Will, you live in that house over there right?" he pointed with his finger. Tori looked around and noticed just across the street was her house. Tori had never noticed Will lived across the street because Judy would not allow her to play in the front outside, "Your too fresh to play in the front" she would say. When she did play outside it was in the small backyard that was filled with bags of empty beer cans, liquor bottles and trash. She would take her only barbie with her and pretended it was her sister. Standing there on there on the sidewalk she noticed her house was the only one that looked run down.

A screeching sound came from the screen door and when it swung open Will screamed "Hi Grandmama Dodie!"

"Boy what you and this girl doing out of school early?"

Wills Grandmother whom he called Dodie was a big sound woman, she had long straight silver hair and a soft round shaped face. Dodie's eyes were deep brown and warm, almost like she was smiling at you through her eyes. Seeing the unkempt condition little Tori was in she bathed her in the tub. After her bath, Tori sat still in the chair while she combed out her matted hair and put two fresh pig tail braids. Dodie spoke in a sweet loving voice telling Tori how beautiful she was and that she would be okay. Dodie told her she would go have a talk with her foster mother and that she could stay at her house that night. They ate pizza for dinner and Dodie made fresh cookies for them while they watched movies. Spending time over Wills house made Tori feel like she had a family.

Ever since then Will was her best friend. When she went home the next day her Foster mother did not say a word to her. From then on, her foster mother stopped beating Tori and would send her to Dodie's house on weekends and for the holidays. On the day Tori turned 18 her foster mother told her to go find her own place to live, she had done her job. Child protective Services were no longer paying her living expenses and she couldn't afford another mouth to feed. Judy had set all of her belongings in trash bags on the porch and changed the locks. Somehow, she was adopting another child and they were coming in a few days. Tori asked Will is she could stay at his place until she landed on her feet. Deep down Tori knew her real mother wouldn't have thrown her out on the street over nothing. As she waited at the bus stop with her trash bags, she promised herself she would find her blood family. Tori stayed on couches and shelters for almost three years. By the time she was 21 she had her own place, a steady job and had enrolled in college majoring in English and Drama. Tori paid through college by working with Will, helping him establish his car dealership. Since she's been in California, she hasn't seen Will in nearly three years. Her finances were becoming overwhelming and it seemed like her life was at a standstill. Something had to change. She was in survival mode and had very little time to figure things out before she ran out of money. It broke her heart if she didn't have money to search for her family. All she wanted to do was find her blood.

Vanessa Robinson

~Tori~

How Does It Feel

I stared at my closet door my name was painted on the back of it in red with the shape of a stiletto around it. Nothing about that symbol represented me, I couldn't find the peace sign so I settled on the shoe. Everyone that meant something to me seemed to walk out of my life anyway so maybe it did fit me. I walked in my closet to pick out something sexy to wear to the impromptu work meeting later. clothes were spread everywhere on the floor. After trying on four different outfits I finally decided on something simple. A white tank top, blazer, ripped jeans and pumps. I didn't want to look too uptight. More than anything I needed to relax; I had the Jacuzzi tub filling up for a bath. I pull of my robe and flip on my iPod music and on comes D'Angelo. Immersing myself in the steamy water I thought about his naked body standing there going in circles on the video. His sweet voice crooning in my ear telling me how much he wanted to feel me, it made me hungry for sex. The melody made me feel hot inside, fire rose from my pussy beneath the water. I positioned my legs open and put my feet up against the side of the tub wall making a clear path for the jets pressure to stimulate me. I turned up the jets with my free hand and other hand stroking my clit. The pressure rushed me turning my fire in a storming California blaze. I closed my eyes and imagined D' Angelo behind me caressing my titties, his hands creeping down my body grabbing my pussy. Diving in hard, then soft going deliberately slow and then fast. Imagining his tender juicy lips on my neck trailing down my back and around to my stomach. His head underwater stroking me with his tongue deep inside gliding against my walls. I laid my head back against the tub day. I could fantasize all day but I needed real love. The tub fantasies just weren't enough anymore.

After my bath I applied my make-up, rolled my hair up and turned on the central air to stay cool while I dressed. I sat at the bar in the living room to put my shoes on and the phone rang. I looked at the phone and wondered who could be calling from an unknown number, on the fourth ring I picked up. I answered in a happy upbeat voice in case it was one those button-down nosey people from work. I told them I was working from home today and to call if they needed anything, but I literally didn't mean that shit.

"Hello, Tori speaking" I chimed. The voice on the other end didn't respond and I was about to hang up. I didn't have time for games on the phone. I said "Hello" once more.

A deep voice replied "What's up sexy, I have something for them perky ass panties you put on today."

Oh shit, it was Will. My heart nearly jumped out of my body at his voice on the line. I needed this phone call, he had perfect timing. Almost like he knew I was thinking of him, I damn sure needed a friend right now. He always said the right words to make me laugh and I missed having him around to hang with more than ever. Back at home as teenagers we'd chill on his grandmother's steps smoke a little weed and just watch the world move. Will's grandmother would throw down on some curry chicken and rice, you could smell it down the street. Neighbors would come to buy plates and stand around the porch eating. We would be high as shit eating and laughing at nothing, it was one big family. Will was a jokester and I was his partner in crime. I missed his company; our world was different then.

"Aye I know you didn't hang up on me, Tori?" I realized I was caught up in my thoughts reminiscing on old times.

"No, I'm still here Will, what's up? I miss you, where have you been? I haven't heard from you in almost 6 months, what's been going on with you?" I rushed him with questions hoping that he wouldn't ask me too much about my life, or exactly how I was doing so I wouldn't break down. It's been sometime since we last talked and I didn't want to burden him with Tori issues.

Will laughed nervously, "Well damn sweetheart I been well. I decided to make the move you always told me I should make and expand the car dealership to the west coast. Business is good out here and I'm trying to shake things up and build the brand." I could tell there was a smile on his face as he spoke by the sound of his voice, he was happy and excited with his life. I had heard from a distant friend that the luxury car dealership he owned was popular statewide and business was booming. I had even bought my own car, a BMW from his dealership before I left home.

"Damn you're doing your thing, you sound good, I'm proud that you're handling your shit."

"Yeah, you know I am all about the paper but that's not the only reason why I called. I wanted to ask you something- "

I wondered what it could be and I replied sharply "What's up? Make it quick, I am on a tight schedule and I don't want to be late, I have a meeting."

"Alright Tori will you marry me?" Will said jokingly.

"Don't play with me, come on Will, I don't think your finance Laura would appreciate you asking me something like that even as a joke. How is she anyways? When am I going to get an invitation for the wedding?"

"I'm just fucking with you. I just wanted to let you know that I'm moving out to Cali in a few weeks, my condo won't be ready until at least three months, so I'm going to need a place to stay for the time being" Will stuttered "So can I stay with you?"

I didn't know if I should laugh or cry. I was stunned, what was I supposed to say? I should say "Yes" but I didn't want to act too excited like I needed him or wanted him close to me. The truth was I did need Will. I've been struggling with my bills and the male company would be nice. I could use Wills help to finish renovating the house and use the extra money to catch up on bills. Then I could take more time to write at home. I pondered how his stuck-up fiancé Laura would feel about this, if he did move in. When I lived in Boston, every time I came around, she would always cut her eyes at me and complain about her man sticking up under me. She'd say shit to me in her Texas accent like "Why yawl so close like that?" Or say to Will "What's so damn funny? Everything that girl say ain't funny." I can't stand a jealous bitch; she'd do anything she could to keep Will on her fingertips and away from me. I realized I was zoning out on Will and hadn't given him an answer yet. I was so nervous I didn't know what to say next. I couldn't get the yes out of my mouth.

"Oh, Will I'm sorry my phone was in and out, must be the yard work they're are doing next door. Will you know you are always welcome for as long as you need. There will be rules here and it won't be for free either, never the less, I have your back." I said firmly.

"Thank you I'll pull my weight while I'm there and some. I just thought instead of spending money in a hotel for about three months I could just pay you and my place will probably be ready before then" Will explained.

"Yeah, I'm cool with that. So, when do you think you will be coming down here?" I asked.

Vanessa Robinson

"I'll probably be down in about two weeks, hopefully a little bit earlier, is that okay with you Miss Tori?" Will said.

"Wait Will, what about Dodie and Laura? Is she okay with you staying with me? Is she coming with you?" I asked.

Inside I was praying that he would say no and she was keeping her ass at home. That girl was rude and she never liked me. I didn't want her here watching my every move.

"Look Tori, honestly Laura and I broke up a few months ago, I broke off the engagement with her and we aren't speaking at all. She did some disrespectful stuff to me and had me in a bind, but I don't want to get into it right now—" His voice trailed off and he was quiet.

"So, you two are done? It's over for real this time?"

"Yeah its done, single as a pringle."

"Dude there is nothing single about that chip, it comes in a stack!"

"I see you still have to always be politically correct."

"Whatever, I'm not letting anything slide with you, you always been a player."

"I'm on my grown man shit right now, I don't have time for the ladies. Besides the ladies ain't showing my love right now."

"How is Dodie doing?"

"Dodie is happy for me; she thinks I need the change of scenery. Dodie's on her old lady shit, she wants to come here and gamble, she has Las Angeles and Las Vegas confused. She met some man at bingo she has been saying she's ready for a sleepover and I need to get out. This old lady is driving me crazy. My boy Chris is going to keep an eye out on her while I'm gone, she isn't as quick on her feet like she thinks. On a serious note, Tori this is something I have to do. I want to make sure when I have a family that they have nothing to worry about, I have to secure the future, you know?" His tone was sincere.

"Yeah, I know Will, I'm sorry about you Laura, I know that you love that crazy girl. Give Dodie a kiss for me and see you in a few weeks."

I hung up the phone and just sat there with my hand on top of it. Waves of electricity pulsed through me; I knew it was the anxiety coming back. My words were robotic when I said that last sentence to Will. I didn't care about him and Laura's relationship because I knew it wasn't a right fit from the beginning. I was relieved my friend was moving on from that toxic relationship.

In a ten-minute conversation my life has just changed. It could be a guarantee that my financial situation was going to get better. I wouldn't have to worry as much or ask my best friend Mae for a loan. I knew she was good for it but she always made it seem like she had to come around more since I had a debt with her. Wills extra money would help pay off some old debts and allow me some breathing room but I knew It wasn't going to be simple. My palms were sweating thinking about both Will and I being single in the same house and sexual tension growing. Now that Laura is out of the picture, Will might want to finish off our little teenage rendezvous, which I can't allow to happen. I am going to have to stand my ground and keep my legs together tight. I don't even want to hug him it's been so long since I've been touched. Our friendship needs to be a hands-off level.

I grabbed my keys, purse and headed to the front door. I could hear the phone ring again as I headed towards my car. "Shit who could be calling now when I'm already heading out." I ran back into the house and picked up the phone.

"Hello?" I yelled, out of breath and annoyed.

"Well Damn! Hello to you too, girl what the hell you so mad about?" It was Mae, my best friend on the line. Irritation was settling in because I told her I wouldn't be home, but she called the house phone anyway.

In my most irritated voice I said, "What bitch? I'm not mad, but I've been trying to leave this house for two hours now. Is this an emergency?"

Mae spoke in a playful voice, "No silly, I just wanted to say hey."

"Well hey, I just not too long ago hung up the phone with Will."

"Who?"

"Mae remember I told you about him? My old boyfriend Will is going to be moving in with me temporarily can you fucking believe it?"

"Damn stop screaming in my ear. So you said Will, your old boo is coming to live with you? Are you serious? Is he bringing his future wife with him too? Why is he coming anyway?"

Mae sounded jealous and curious at the same time, asking questions that were not her business. I explained to her he will be here soon and that him and Laura broke up but he hadn't told me why. I told her he was coming to check out some new opportunities in California. It was none of her business but I knew she was going to keep fishing around for more information. Mae was one of the nosiest people I knew, nothing could get past her. If she couldn't get information she would turn into a private investigator.

"Oh, so are you thinking about getting back with him or fucking him?" Mae said.

"No Mae, I'm past that, as-a-matter-of fact we are JUST friends, he's like family. You sound a little mad I'm getting a roommate and it's not you." I knew she would get annoyed and want to get off the phone.

"Whatever, I'm your best friend, you don't have to run that bullshit on me. You know you want some bid D. I think you low key want a man. You can't tell me Tori that you won't fuck him if he tries you" She said knowingly.

I was appalled and pissed off now.

"I need to go somebody's calling in." I threw my phone in my purse. Who the hell did she think she was telling me what I was feeling or thinking? I can't stand when she tries to fuck with my energy. I didn't want him. I had my fantasies and that was it. Finally, I left my house and headed out to my car. Traffic was the usual bumper to bumper, but I lived close to the jazz restaurant I was heading to. My cell phone vibrated in my purse and of course it was Mae calling me back, probably pissed I hung up in her face. I answered the phone "What?"

She jumped right in, "Oh, come on Tori, I'm just letting you know what I think, not trying to sound like a bitch. I just want to see you happy. You're my homegirl and I care about you." Mae explained.

"Okay thanks, but I think I know what I need more than you do. Your opinion is based off the past and I don't care to hear it." I said.

Mae let out a sigh on the other end. "So, I'll see you tonight? Let's have drinks at my place or your place."

"Be at my place by eleven on the fucking dot" I screamed into the phone and hung up.

I had more to focus on, I had written a manuscript and my Literary agent and I were meeting with a publisher. We wanted to see what kind of deal he had to offer and I wanted to make sure I had my mind right. I pulled up and said a quick prayer. I walked slowly to the door concentrating on my negotiation skills. Just looks were going to get me a good deal. Having something was better than nothing but in truth, I wanted it all.

I opened the door and was greeted by my Literary Agent Dru, she reminded me of a female version of Idris Elba. Dru wore her hair short and her skin dark like night. When she smiled her teeth shined like pearls. I hadn't seen her in months and it looked like she was hitting the gym. Dru's shoulders were built broad and legs hard and strong. She carried herself in a masculine way and wore men's clothes. Whenever we were together most people referred to her as Sir because her breast were small and well hidden. When she laid eyes on me, she smiled, her arms went around the small of back and she placed a simple kiss on my cheek. Dru had on a spicy cologne and it seemed to make me shiver inside, gosh she smelled good. Dru had a way of making me feel like I was the only woman in the room, she was the perfection combination of charming and sweet. Her aurora exuded romance that drew into her. If only I could find someone that took so much pride in themselves. Dru grabbed my hand and confidently led me to the table to prepare to meet with the publisher so we could seal the deal.

~Mae~

Girls Trip

If Tori could see the plans that I have for her she'd run half way across the world from me. Twice she hung up the phone in my face, it turned me on when she worked herself up. I laid back on the couch to hatch a plan for the ultimate seduction. Many lonely nights I've dreamed about resting my head on her pillow soft firm breast. I wanted to try her bad. When I first met Tori on the plane, I couldn't resist her. She was traveling to California with an absurd amount of luggage looking sad. I sat next to her on the layover in Atlanta and it was an instant connection. I chatted her up about all the good places to see in Cali and made sure she took my number so I could be her tour guide. Wherever we went, I took pictures of her for my photography portfolio and that's when I noticed how beautiful she was. plump lips, her soft, smooth brown skin, long, curly black, wild natural hair, and big bambino eyes. Tori is smart, witty, cunning and classy all at once, she could set fire to wood just by breathing on it. Last month my therapist told me my obsession with her wasn't healthy and I needed to stop. I cussed that bitch out and told her she was fired. Tonight, is the night to seduce her, I've been waiting on this opportunity for years. Hopefully after this she will see that we are perfect together. I'm going to make sure no one intervenes and cancel out those old feelings she might have for Will. Will hasn't met me yet but I'm going to find out every last one of his dirty secrets and expose him to Tori.

I was for sure Tori was a straight woman, but sometimes I wonder about her sexuality. In the beginning of our friendship she established she was still finding herself but she never came out and said if she would try having a relationship with another woman.

I wanted to tell her I was into her but there never seemed to be the right time to say it. The way she stares into my eyes, like a lover's stare maybe it's just me overthinking. I remember last summer we went on a girl's trip to Jamaica. On the first night we partied at the resort club and back at the room we drank until we could barely walk. Our suite led out to a balcony and was lit up by candles with the moon shining in. We grooved the whole night long to old school jams. We talked shit, joked and laughed about dances I used to do back in New

Vanessa Robinson

York City when I was a dancer. The drinks were flowing that night and we had smoked a little of that fire Jamaican weed. At the mini bar I poured a glass of wine and accidently bumped into Tori and the red liquid spilled on my cleavage. Tori apologized and when I reached for a towel, she stepped closer to me. I could feel her breath on my skin. Tori whispered in a husky tipsy voice "Now I know you aren't going to let that go to waste" as she looked in my eyes. She stuck her fingertips between my breast bringing her fingers to her lips, sucking it off. I was totally shocked and turned on at the same time. Instantly my nipples were hard and my pussy was hotter than a New Orleans summer day. I was turned on, her name escaped out my mouth, she was teasing me. I grabbed Tori by the waist and kissed her sexy soft juicy lips. I didn't expect Tori to kiss me back but her tongue went deep into my mouth and our lips wrestled each other. I swallowed Tori's tongue over and over, each time her tongue seemed to dissolve into my mouth like candy. I slowly rubbed and gently squeezed her round ass making my way to her hungry pussy. It was getting hot in the room, my fingers entwined with the sweat on her lower back. I knew she was wasted but the timing was perfect. I palmed her breast and I could feel her nipple rising like little hard cherries. Just as I was reaching under her mini skirt to indulge in her seeping wet panties, she suddenly pulled away from me. She looked at me and her eyes looked lost as if she didn't know who I was or even herself. Tori smiled at me and spoke a little above a whisper

"Girl we need to stop drinking, what the hell are we doing?" she laughed turned her back to me and kept talking. "I am never drinking again, Mae this shit is way out of my league". She sounded so sober in that moment, then she went on and on rambling about how she couldn't be a lesbian. I nodded my head and agreed with her that things just went left.

I was guilty for taking advantage of her. I knew I had to play the innocent card or she could be done with me as a friend. I jumped in on her rambling and said, "Look Tori, I'm sorry. I guess it's the alcohol I've never done this before, but hey look on the bright side I'm not some stranger, I'm your best friend and this is between me and you. You're a good kisser Tori."

Although my speech was slurred, I think she knew what I meant. We then both burst out laughing at each other, Tori complained about being too tired and drunk to keep her eyes open. I helped her take off her heels and started cleaning up. When I came back from the trash compactor, she had passed out on the bed in just her boy shorts with no bra. I watched her sleep and played out the events that had just transpired in the last hour over and over in my mind. I had kissed many women before but something about hers was different, we had a connection. I finished the last of the liquor on the deck in the fresh air watching the waves. I had Tori's damp thong in my hand to my nose smelling her sweet essence. It was just a matter of time; nothing was going to stop me from getting this sweet pussy. Tori belonged to me I wasn't going to let anyone have her.

Her Blood

~Tori~

Drinks on me

After my appointment with my agent Dru, I was still didn't know if I would get stable. My mind was not at ease, I had no idea how I would pay my mortgage. We didn't come to a deal about the script and I needed to get my house ready for Will. I cleaned out the office and moved the computer to the gym room. I put clean sheets on the queen size bed to cover my discretions when I first moved in. I finished off the guest room with some blue curtains. I tried to make the room as comfortable as possible for him. My bedroom was in the loft upstairs and the guestroom was on the first floor in the back of the house. We actually did not have to cross paths if we needed to. Will would have access to his own bathroom and separate entrance to the kitchen. The back bedroom also had its own patio that led to the garage and garden.

I was exhausted from cleaning, I knew I told Mae to come at eleven O'clock and if I cancel on her, she'd probably cuss me out. I was not in the mood for an argument. I just hope when she comes, she doesn't bring me down memory lane with William. I need someone in my life now but it definitely wasn't him. We dated for a short time and on the surface everything was perfect. He was spontaneous, sweet, charming and always made me laugh. The way his arms wrapped around me after a long day made me feel whole again and loved. I would catch myself smiling for no particular reason or laughing by myself sometimes at the thought of something funny he'd said. Our friendship goes back to childhood and I looked up to him, he was my anchor.

Our relationship was short but Will and I didn't stop having sex until the day I left Boston. Wills bedroom loving triggered every nerve in my body. He had a way of keeping me aroused even when he wasn't around. Rolling over in the morning finding his face smiling would make me feel warm and angelic inside. There was a downside to our relationship. He had lied to me about a lot of things and I found out he was dating Laura at the same time. Things were getting serious between us and I wanted him to choose. I was young back then but I knew I was worth more than being cheated on. He was out of control with the cheating and I couldn't take it anymore. Will tried to fix what we had done by breaking it off with Laura but he still had other women on the side. I couldn't compromise my happiness with that fuckery. I decided that Will should just be a friend, nothing more than that. I promised myself I would never go back on my word no matter what he presented to me.

I was folding the last bit of blankets when the phone rang. I wasn't in the mood for talking so I let it ring until it stopped. There was a text it from Will: "Change of plans, I'm going to be heading up there this weekend to look at some property is that okay with you?" Wow, I wasn't expecting that, I waited a few minutes to text him back.

As I sat there my stomach starting doing somersaults at the thought of seeing his charming smile. Luckily, I'd already cleaned out the spare bedroom, my phone went off again another text from Will, "The contractors need me out there by Monday morning, I'm looking to sign a lease for office spaces and a garage. My manager moved some things up for me, I'm sorry to inconvenience you, I will make it up to you" the text read.

I replied "It's okay if you come, let me know when your plane lands and I will send a car" I tried to keep the text as short as possible. I didn't want to carry out the conversation. I called Mae to see where she was at, she picked up the phone on the first ring saying "Hello" in a rushed voice.

Her Blood

"Hey girl, where are you? You're late as usual" I said.

"I will be there in a minute, I had to pick up --" before she could finish her sentence I spilled out "Will is coming this weekend girl, he has some business to handle and needs to come ASAP so--"

Mae cut me off "So what about our plans tonight? It's supposed to be you and me this weekend."

"Hold on Mae I don't recall us making plans for the whole weekend. We made plans for tonight, only right? I'm not going to indulge too much or smoke that crazy Jamaican shit you have. I'm just going to chill out. The last thing I need is a hangover. I don't want my head spinning like character from a Marvel movie in the morning" I said.

Mae abruptly hung up the phone and a few minutes later there she was banging on the door. When I opened the door, she stood with a disappointed look on her face, her lips were all poked out. She pushed passed me and ordered me to grab the bags out of the car in the driveway. I took three bags out of the trunk full of wine, vodka and Thai food. I stopped to clear my mind and take in a view of the outside garden for a minute. Everything out here seemed to be immaculate. The garden was full of red and yellow roses and life size lilies that I had planted myself. I had a baby weeping willow tree planted in the middle and a waterfall made of rocks next to the swinging white bench. I bought the antique bench because it reminded me of Dodie rocking back and forth on it. When I was little in the mornings, she'd watch the kids skip off to school. It made me feel comfortable, like an angel was watching over me making sure I was safe. Now I lived on top of a hill and the whole city lay beneath the hill like blanket with the mountains shadowing over. Gazing at the life cycles of nature took away the uneasiness that filled me.

I took in a few long deep breaths, a walked back into the house. Mae was laid back on the long suede lounge chair next to the window. She was sipping a pink colored liquor out of one of my tall crystal glasses. Mae was exotic looking like Nicole murphy but with curly long black hair, her skin glistened like the sun had set in it. Mae had brown amber eyes the same as me except hers had a hint of green. No man could resist her round ass and long toned legs. Every event we attended we received VIP treatment because of her popularity and stunning beauty. I wasn't about to kiss her ass after getting on my nerves.

Her Blood

After staring at me with an evil look on her face Mae finally spoke. In a curt tone she said "Took you long enough, the drinks were getting warm." She had calmed down from her tantrum this morning. I ran over to her and gave her a hug and a kiss on both cheeks.

"I miss my bestie what's up?" as I walked into the kitchen to grab a cork. Mae followed ignoring my question. She reached in her purse and pulled out a blunt fatter than a porn stars dick, rolled to perfection and lit it.

I was shocked "Damn are you trying to put me in a coma! I am not smoking all that! We are not smoking all that!" I screamed.

Mae fired back, "Shut the hell up scary ass! All we need is a little bit anyway. Trust me when you hit this shit right here, you'll be walking on cloud nine. We can just relax and explore our minds."

"I don't know about all that exploration shit you're talking about; we are not under the sea girl."

"You take life too serious Tori; you need to let loose sometimes. All the shit you have going on, ain't going nowhere. Learn to enjoy yourself sometimes."

Thinking about what she said maybe it wouldn't be such a bad idea to think about something else for a change. I needed to take my mind off Will coming and worrying if this screen play deal would go through or not. I didn't like the look on her face though, she looked like she had something up her sleeve. Mae was standing there grinning and already looking high and tipsy. She relit the blunt, took a hard pull and then passed it to me. When I inhaled the smoke my throat burned instantly, on the second pull my face and throat went numb. I tried to hold it in but I ended up coughing. After my choking episode, I started to feel a haze over me. my body was glued to the chair for a second. If my head could of detached like a balloon I'm for sure it would have flown off if I didn't lean forward. I wanted to throw up but my lunch stayed in my throat. I watched Mae make us two cocktails the glass filled with half grey goose and just a drop of cranberry juice. When she noticed me watching her our eyes met and a half-crooked grin came over her full red lips. She stood up and motioned for me to follow her, we both walked down my long narrow hallway to the living room that was full of pillows. I designed the living room for relaxation, the floor was actually a down bed with built in tables. A small bar was built in the wall and on the opposite side of the room was a seventy-five -inch TV. We both sat next to the bar and laid back to watch the classic movie already playing Set It Off.

One hour had passed and I was feeling toasted, my mind was cloudy. I had smoked half of the blunt and had more than four of Mae's heavy drinks she kept pouring. My legs had become Japanese noodles and my honey pot was throbbing. Scenes of cuddling against a big strong man and doing some serious fuckin was racing through my mind. But then I remembered for the last year my bed has been empty and I've only had fun nights with my bullet. My king bed just had me in it, when I carried myself up to the loft tonight, I would just have to make the bullet work. I wanted to go upstairs and go to bed but my body couldn't move. The room seemed to be spinning like I was on a fast merry-go-round.

While I was daydreaming and reminiscing off the many nights I spent with my bullet and former lovers, Mae lay next to me with her hands running through my hair. She caressed my scalp hitting the sore spots releasing the tension. I leaned into Mae's shoulder resting my head on her right breast, I could hear the muzzle drum beats of her heart. She wore a low-cut top and her skin was glowing. Mae ran her hand over my face, her fingertips brushing down my skin. She planted small kisses on my forehead, down my nose then onto my cheeks. I laid there watching the TV. I always wanted to play the Jada Pinkett in the set if off movie, she smart. They were robbing the last bank heading for disaster, that bitch made it out with all the money. I was on a different planet. I was high than I'd ever been in my entire life. My mind was at ease, relation had kicked in. As if I were playing a role in my own movie, I could see myself outside my own body. I found myself grabbing Mae's face and kissing her cheeks, the same way she kissed me. My mouth ended up on hers and somehow, we were entwined in a passionate tongue kiss. Her tongue wrestling with mine with her hand on the back of my neck pulling me in closer, her tongue going deep. I was high, horny and my pussy was desperately dripping wet. I couldn't stop. Mae touched my body all over while our tongues made love, her lips travelled to my neck and then onto my breast. Her lips wrapped around my nipples, sucking them in and out of her mouth over and over. A trail of kisses down to my belly button with her hands now around my hips. Mae slid off my pants and thong in one motion. She spread my legs, grabbed both of them and dove in between. Her lips grab onto my clit, my pussy was dripping wet and her mouth was hot. Her warm tongue was like ice on my fire, she hungrily licked and sucked me, catching every drop of my wetness. I stated to throw my pussy into her mouth feeding her and she moaned each time I creamed into her mouth, swallowing every bit. I started to orgasm without my permission over and over. Each time my hips would buck into the air and I would nearly faint the jerk move. Mae made circles with her mouth pulling me in and out, she teased my pussy and inner thigh, and then she would go back to greedily sucking my swollen clit. Her arms wrapped around my legs tight so I could not break free. I didn't know if I was dreaming or not, it was good and wrong at the same time. I was couldn't believe what my body was making me do. Another orgasm was coming... I garnered every bit of strength I had to scream. I screamed so loud Mae stopped and asked if I was okay. I quickly slid out of her grasp to the other side of the bed and grabbed for my panties.

I was so confused, as I grabbed my clothes off the floor, I tried to say no but I couldn't speak. My mouth full of cotton and pangs of body weakness flowed through me with every movement. Mae sat in front of me waving her hands, saying my name, asking "Are you okay?" and the rest sounded like gargle noises. My voice wouldn't cooperate with my thoughts. She sounded far away; I was over the top high. Panic set in, my heart beating fast in my chest. "I need to get out of here." I crawled up the loft stairs into the bathroom and locked the door. Mind was racing over what just happened. I held onto the bathroom sink and began to stand with one knee up and vomit came up my mouth. I threw up over and over, the only thing that came up was alcohol. I turned on the water in the tub to ice cold and jumped in. Mae was banging on the door and twisting the knob trying to get in. As the cold water filled around my naked body, a tinge of calm came over me. My mind began to wake up, bringing the high down. I had to get out of the daze I was in. I realized I couldn't just leave her out there and decided to answer, but there was no way I was opening the door. I was too embarrassed and confused to face her. "Mae I'm too out if right now, you should just go home, I'm sorry." My voice was raspy and I knew she could hear in my voice I didn't want to see her. She stood there for a few minutes listening. There was an eerie silence aside from the running water. I heard her walk down the steps slowly and then slam the front door hard. Her car started up and the tires screeched loudly as she pulled off.

Her Blood

The round thin edges of the tub suffocated underneath my buttocks while I tried to gain my bearings. I was weak. The wind was knocked out of me and my head was pounding, I could barely see a few feet in front me. I can't understand how just a few cocktails could make me feel so hungover. My legs were wobbly so I slid myself down each of the steps to the living room. My place was a mess, there were glasses half full of wine clothes strewed on the floor, and it smelled like Mary Janes aftertaste. Mae's bra was thrown over the couch, I could've sworn she was fully dressed last night. The whole room looked like a dream I wish I never had. I couldn't put the events together in my mind of how I ended up so intoxicated and high enough to fuck my best friend. In my right mind I would never do that. If I ever thought about experimenting with a woman it wouldn't have been with Mae, we were too close. Mae was too raunchy. On the chair there was her overnight bag opened up and I could see my blouse she had borrowed from me a few weeks ago sticking out. I grabbed my shirt out of the bag and a small plastic vile rolled out onto the floor. I wasn't sure what it was but it was filled with a coffee brown colored liquid. I popped off the top, it had a stench like ganga water and ammonia. I dead bolting the doors and brought it upstairs with me along with my cell phone. I already had four missed calls and a text from Mae claiming she left her bag. I didn't have the energy to respond back. As I lay on my pillow I just cried, I didn't know who I was anymore. My best friend or so I thought, just had sex with me and I couldn't explain why I liked it or how I allowed it to happen. Tears rolled onto my pillow, the heaviness set in.

I opened my eyes and immediately I knew then it was seven o'clock in the morning. Same time every morning my foster mother would wake me up with a slap in the face to go to school. Judy didn't like to repeat herself, when she screamed "Wake up!" at my bedroom door she wasn't going to say it again. After the first couple times I started expecting it, it turned me from a deep sleeper as a child to being able to hear a pin drop through my dreams. I sat up out of the bed and put my feet on the floor and tried to stand. Weakness lingered all through me this was the worst hangover I've ever had. I pushed myself to stand and begin to clean up the mess in the house. Every time I bent down, whatever was in my stomach was rising up. This wasn't a typical dried out, small headache hangover. I turned on my phone to google some type of remedy but I had twelve missed calls. Majority of them were from Mae but there was three from Will. I forgot he told me he was coming this weekend. Here it was Friday and I was a complete mess. I just wanted to get back in bed, cuddle with my blanket and recover from last night but I knew it would be impossible with Will coming today. I couldn't let him see me looking crazy or like something was bothering me. The pit of my stomach was twisting and turning, I had to eat to get my day started. I made an egg white omelet with spinach. I dialed Wills phone, he answered on the first ring.

"Tori what's going on? My plane landed a half an hour ago!" Will said, yelling at me. I was shocked and immediately a burning sensation harbored in my chest.

"Oh my gosh! I will send a car. Will, I'm so sorry I had a long night and slept in."

"You don't sound like yourself, are you good?" he said concerned.

"I'm feel fine, I'm alright." I tried to say it in my most assuring voice but I knew I wasn't sure about anything. He started rambling about how the flight took longer due to the crowds at the airport. I was somewhat listening, but I was more worried about my health. I put my phone on mute an immediately texted my Doctor's nurse and explained my symptoms. She texted back asking me to come into the office as soon as possible. I hung up the phone with Will and ran into the shower. I washed my hair and scrubbed every part of me that Mae touched. I had a gut feeling that something was wrong with me. I made sure I packed the stinky vile in my purse, I snatched the blunt out of the ashtray that she was smoking on the lounge chair.

I arrived at the doctor's office and when she walked out, she shook her head at my looks.

"You look a tired, have you been getting any rest."

"I had a long night."

"What is it that you have for me today? You mentioned that you're sick or you took something?"

"I think--, I might have. I just want to know what this is and what it does?"

I pressed down on my right leg to stop it from shaking while she drew my blood and collected a sample from the obscure vile.

"Tori your blood pressure is raised, I can tell your worried about something. Do you want to explain to me what happened?"

Silence.

"Okay, how did you get possession of this?" she pointed to the container.

"I don't know if I was drugged last night but I was really out of it and I didn't drink that much. I was with a friend."

"If you have a so-called friend that you have to worry about giving you something without your knowledge, I suggest you stay away from that friend."

Hands trembled as I held onto the prescription for nausea and anxiety.

"Get some rest, and make sure you eat, I will notify you within a few days with the results.

I sat outside of the medical office building in my car watching people walk in a hurry trying not to miss their appointments. I wondered if any of them were going through what I had been through last night. I checked my phone and I had four missed calls from Mae, I wasn't ready to talk with her yet. I knew if I didn't answer in a few days she would up at house and use the key I gave her for emergencies. I didn't want her just showing up and now that Will was staying here. I didn't want him to know about what happen last night.

Driving home, I realized it could be possible that Mae could have drugged me and took advantage of me. She always wanted to spend more time together than usual and I would often beg her to find other things to do than to hang with me. We'd spend every weekend together and after a few weekends in a row I'd be so tired. Tired of getting high with her and her endless rambling. I'd feel drained and pretend I was busy the following weekend just to get alone time to myself. She would be so persistent to hang out more, I would try to avoid her. In the back of my mind I always wondered why she wasn't concerned with the man she said she had. Since I have known her, she supposedly had the same guy, but I never met him. She never told me his name or anything too much about him. I started to think he wasn't real but as time passed because she never gave details. It was just I have a man and that's it. I never had the time to put any clues together. I was so consumed with work and my struggle. I had projects with deadlines and I figured I was being overreactive and silly to think my friend would make up something like that. Looking back from the time we met years ago to now, some things she told me don't add up. If it was built on a lie, it would make more sense. Trying to wrap my head around it made me feel so lost. I know I have to sort it out so I can be at ease. Thinking back to our trip to Jamaica when she kissed me and tried to seduce me, I just blamed everything on the alcohol taking over. That trip, makes me wonder what her intentions were in being my friend. I love my best friend Mae like a sister, but something is telling me after last night she might feel differently. A ball of confusion was rising up inside my throat. I had to figure out why she did this to me.

I pulled into my driveway, there was a black Lincoln parked. I could tell by the silhouette through the window that it was Will. I parked beside the driver's car, taking in a few slow deep breaths. Will opened his door and stepped out with a beer in his hand and arms spread open wide. The top was down on my car and I could hear him saying "Hey baby I'm here." Damn he looked so good. His skin had a touch of bronze that was deep chocolate colored brown. His skin was so perfect in the sun and his eyes were round shaped with the mature creases at the end. He had a thin mustache on his top lip just enough to give your pussy a little tingle. His beard wrapped around his face like black winter blanket and he had high cheek bones and full puffy pink lips. His eyebrows were thick and his lineup was perfect. His face and build were perfectly sculpted. Will looked like he worked out in the gym every day, he stood six feet and some odd inches with broad strong shoulders. His muscles were round, he carried a football player build. Wills smile was crooked like he was having nasty thoughts while he watched me walk up. I knew he wanted to fuck me on site. I was not going to let that happen.

I slowly walked into Will embrace and he wrapped his big arms around my waist and hugged me tightly. Will had on a strong sweet musty cologne. As I inhaled in his arms, it tingled my nose and ran through my body. It was a musty and sweet aroma just as I remembered. He did always like to make you remember him when he entered the room, whether it was his irresistible smile or scent.

After the tight embrace Will followed me into the kitchen staring at my ass making low key whistle noises. I wanted catch up and hopefully lay down some ground rules for his short stay. I showed him the bathroom and guest bedroom he would be using. I pointed to the door that he could use to leave and come in aside from the front entrance. Will and I then sat in the kitchen on the bar stools and I let him know how happy I was that he came. Even if the intention was business it was nice to have a familiar face around.

Her Blood

Will opened his mouth to speak and before he could say anything, I cut him off. "Just business Will, I don't want to revisit the past and get mixed up remising about us, just business and friendship nothing more." I smiled and exhaled at the same time; it was a relief to get that off my chest.

Will spoke in an even tone matching mine "Tori, I am only here to get my business going and nothing more. I promise you I will stay out of your way and respect your house and you. I am pretty happy you let me stay here. This favor saves me a lot of money and hassle of a hotel, you have a nice place here baby girl can you show me around?"

I showed him the lounge room, living room and just pointed to the upstairs where the loft was. I didn't want him to see the loft area where my bedroom was or to get any ideas.

He looked up at the sheer curtain and tea lights on the balcony, pointing upwards "That must be a top-secret area that I can't see huh?" I tried to laugh it off and said sternly, "Yup, no one goes up there but me myself and I!"

A simper smile came over his lips but his eyes had a defeated look that he couldn't see my bedroom. His hand brushed over his abs that were peeking through his tight shirt. "Let's go to dinner." I motioned him toward the kitchen and said "There's a stack of take out menus in the kitchen drawer." I couldn't go to dinner, I had somethings to take care of. Will mumbled something under this breath and walked off into the kitchen. As I made my way to the stairs down the hall, I heard his phone ring. I could hear him talking in the kitchen, I couldn't quite make out what he was saying and doubled back down the hall on my tippy toes. I could tell by the deep aggressiveness in his voice he was talking to another man and it sounded like he said "How many? Alight then I'll pick it up later." I wasn't quite sure what he meant or what exactly he was picking up. As he spoke his voice became lower, almost to a whisper. I inched closer to the kitchen to trying to hear, as I did the hardwood floor creaked underneath my shoes like Dodie's old stairwell. Will stopped talking and abruptly ended the call. I crept up the hallway up to my loft and watched him from an opening in the curtains. He dragged his big suitcase and three other large bags into the back bedroom. Will had rather too many bags for the time he was staying. He was a man of style and loved to wear designer shoes with his clothes, I hope his suitcase was filled with just that.

I was curious to know what exactly Will had going on but eavesdropping wasn't getting me anywhere. I had to put that to the side, my mind needed a break. My energy was drained mentally and emotionally. I climbed up the stairs locking my bedroom door behind me, it was weird having someone else staying in the house. I peeled my clothes off and threw them to the floor like rags. My insides were dirty from last night. I laid back on the bed and grabbed the surround sound remote and put on some soft music. I needed to figure out what happen last night and if that vile I found had anything to do with me feeling so sick. A slight headache was lingering behind my eyes. I was sipping on juice and water all day to stay hydrated as the doctor ordered. In the bed, I laid on my side with my fingers in my hair massaging my scalp trying to release the pain. I stared at my phone screen and I had yet again three more missed calls from Mae. I had my phone on silent the whole day avoiding her. In addition to the calls from Mae, I had two missed calls and a text from Dru. The text from Dru read "Hey beautiful I have some good news for you. I'd like to meet for dinner." I didn't want to text back just yet; I couldn't handle anything else for today. I would reply before the weekend was over. I was so much in my head my mind kept going back to last night. Breaking me out of my zone I heard Will yell out over the music he was stepping out for a minute. I screamed back "Wait!" when I realized that I didn't give him a key. I was naked so I tossed on my black silk robe and ran down the stairs. I grabbed the front door spare key from the foyer table drawer and handed it to him. Will stood there smiling. It was a little funny, the smile he had plastered on his face with his eyebrows going up and down. I looked down at myself and tucked in my left nipple that was peeking out of my robe.

"You should be paying for the peep show you just had" I said playfully.

Will took a step closer "How much you want baby?"

"Don't you have somewhere to be?" I tried to back up, but he had my hand in his with the key still in my mine.

I shot a glance at my hand and pulled slightly, and he let go. A stiff smile came over my face and we just stood there for a few seconds staring into each other eyes saying nothing. Staring at his face I noticed his eyes looked more tired, he had just a few wrinkle lines across his forehead and darkness underneath his eyes. He stared at me so intently almost like he was trying to see through me.

Her Blood

Will broke the silence. "I was just heading out to grab something to eat and meet up with an associate, would you like to join pretty lady?"

"No, I will take a raincheck this time. I'm going to rest up for a run in the morning, don't wake me when you get back."

"Alight cool I will see you later." Will waved, I shut the door and locked it behind him. I looked out the window and saw him walking down around the corner then I heard a car door slam shut and loud music. I could hear it bumping rap music and it trailed off down the street. Somehow, I figured he knew I would say no, and I was not aware he had a rental car delivered. It didn't make sense for him not to have them bring it to my private driveway, but maybe he did not want to block me in. It seemed funny they would have the music up loud like that too.

I went back up to my bedroom and looked at my phone again. There were more missed calls and messages, I didn't want to get back to anyone. I'm too tired for anymore drama. I laid my head back and took deep breath to clear my mind. I closed my eyes and just started repeating "sleep, sleep, sleep" rocking myself back and forth. Finally, the sweet

Vanessa Robinson

feeling of sleep coming over me and my body
sinking into the bed.

Her Blood

Vanessa Robinson

~Mae~

Mr. Fuckin Buick

Two hours. For Two hours I drove around Tori's neighborhood, passing by her house. I circled around the cul-de-sac to see if her bedroom light was on. Each time I passed by her house it was all dark, every window was black. I called her phone nine times and she didn't answer. The last call I made to her phone started going straight to voicemail. I left her four text messages on top of it and still no response. As I was driving home, tears fell from my eyes. I lost her for real this time, she blocked me from communicating with her. I could tell in her voice as she screamed through the door last night that she didn't me around. I had to do something to get her to talk me again, to at least get her to see I love her. I still had the keys to her house for emergencies, the GPS tracking app on my phone showed that her car was still sitting in her driveway. About six months back, I put a tracker on her car after she went out on a date and I couldn't get in touch with her. Most of the time when I'd call Tori and ask where she was, I'd already have an idea since I could see her location. The funniest of things is when she lies to me when she doesn't want to be bothered and says "Oh I'm out and about" and I know she's right at home. I never called her on it, I wouldn't want her to get any hints that I knew where she was. The tracker comes in handy when she is with someone. Some nights when I am missing her, I ride by her place to see if her lights are on or if any cars are in the driveway. Tori rarely has company except for that one time.

One night there was a deep blue Buick parked in her driveway freshly washed. I could see the car sparkling from across the street where I sat ducked down in my driver's seat. The Buick stayed until three in the morning, Tori's bedroom lights were on and the music blasting. My skin crawled every time I saw shadows of their naked bodies in the window, knowing she was inside fuckin'. After two hours, Tori opened the door dressed in a just a robe and her hair scattered over her head. She kissed Mr. Buick deep and slow and then retreated inside the house. I watched as the tall, dark skinned man with muscles bulging out of his shirt. He waltzed down the driveway whistling with his head in the clouds, high off her loving. I followed him at a distance as he drove sloppy on the road, to a broke a hood ass looking neighborhood about thirty minutes away. He pulled into a driveway in front of a house that was falling apart and dark. I parked my car on the street a few cars away. As I walked toward his driveway, I ripped open my shirt busting off three buttons and ruffled up my hair. When he opened his car door, I was in ear shot and began to cry loudly. With tears pouring out of my eyes I yelled, "Mister my boyfriend just threw me out of our car, I've been walking for blocks, can I please use your phone?" My mascara burned my eyes and slid down my cheeks. I know I looked desperate and helpless.

Mr. Buick looked me up and down, his eyes stayed for a long time on my breast. The air kissed my nipple that was sticking out of my shirt, making it curl up into a ball. He had a dirty smirk on his face and his eyes squinted, his words spilled over wet soaked lips in a raspy voice.

"Yeah you can use my phone, come in the house baby its cold out here."

I walked behind him and I could smell the pussy whipped scent coming off him. He opened his front door and I was surprised the inside of his home was immaculate. It was a bachelor pad with mainly black furniture, a huge flat screen television and a gaming system with huge speakers. I asked him to use his bathroom and he directed me to a short hallway off the small white galley kitchen. Looking in the mirror sweat had already beaded around my forehead and down my neck. In my right hand I held onto my knife that my father used to own. I remember him using it the first time he took me fishing when I was 7 years old. He taught me how to gut a fish, the same way he would tear up my insides every time he took me on a daddy daughter trip.

I stared back at my reflection, I was not that unimportant, helpless, little girl anymore, I was powerful now. I cleaned the sweat from head and walked out the bathroom with the knife behind my back. My whole shirt was open now and both my breast were exposed. I walked slow and sexy towards him, my titties bouncing with every motion. Mr. Buick had lit candles and I could smell jasmine incense in the air. As I moved closer, I could see the front of his pants begin to rise. I reached out and grabbed his dick and begin to stroke it through his pants to full erection. I knew I had this freak bastard's attention now. He stared me dead in the eyes licking his lips. I grabbed full hold of his junk and pulled downwards trying to rip it off. I swiftly pulled the knife from behind me with my free hand and stuck it into his neck. Mr. Buick froze up; his eyes were bulging. I spit in his face and it dripped down his cheeks mixing with his tears as I was still pulling on his dick with all my might. I kissed his lips and slid my tongue up face licking the salty tears and spit mixed together. My hand still pulling down hard on his dick and balls. I watched as his eyes rolled back from the pain.

"I know you fucked Tori tonight, you'll never get her again, she's fucking mine!" He shook his head back and forth and choking sound coming out of his mouth as he tried to speak.

I shoved the blade deeper through his throat and slid it up to his chin. I pulled a little harder until his balls detached. Mr. Buicks body fell to the hardwood floor in a bloody mess. He laid there in a heap and I sat on the black leather couch smoking a cigarette. I had no choice to kill this creep, he was just like George, all men were. I took his ID out of his wallet so I could see his name. Mr. Buicks name was Ronnie West. I drove past Tori's house again that night and all the lights were out. I promised I'd never let another person get between us again. After that anyone that she thought was good for her I intervened. I would find a reason to make her believe something that was wrong with them and Tori would take the bait, she trusted me. Tori would end it and we'd be right back to hanging 24/7 again.

Her Blood

Vanessa Robinson

~Will~

No discussion needed

I knew Tori wouldn't go with me to dinner before I even asked her. Tori seemed preoccupied with something on her mind the way she reflected me. Her eyes were dark underneath like she could use some sleep. I called my friend Leon to come pick me up from Tori's place. I gave him the address a couple houses down so Tori couldn't see who I was rolling with. I didn't want her in my shit, she was a smart woman she could spot a drug dealers car from her rearview mirror. If she knew that Leon was a drug dealer, she would have questions for me, I couldn't risk her finding out anything.

Leon pulled up in a brand-new chrome Mercedes with smoke seething out of every window. When I opened the door, I could barely see him in the driver seat puffing off his blunt.

"Damn bro, it's like that!"

"Shit is legal here, get in." He leaned back in his seat and sped off.

"Where's that fine ass girl you staying with, I bet she has that organic pussy huh?"

"Yeah whatever, just drive and pass me the blunt! We cool ain't shit going on with that!"

"Will you ain't getting no pussy and you've been in jail! I have something for you at the crib. I got you homie." Leon turned up the music and the speakers rattled every panel on the car in unison with the beats.

Leon's living room couch didn't have any legs. My knees made a funny noise when I sat down. Every piece of furniture in the room was torn, broken or full of cigarette burns like the furniture itself were the life of the party. There were two young Mexican girls with black pencil thin eyes brows sitting at the kitchen table bagging crack. In-between giggling and collecting small rocks out of a metal pan they bent down every so often to snort a line. I could tell they were already high and both barely looked eighteen years old. They girls were dressed in tiny shorts and their t-shirts barely covered their breast. I knew Leon was into some weird shit but I didn't know he was into young prostitutes. Leon always kept women and girls around him that he could get high and do whatever he wanted with. He was the kind of man that you knew not to say no to. Leon had people working for him that would kill for him and his money stacked. I asked him for a favor and even though I knew he was good for it; he would have me in his back pocket. I'd have to do whatever he asked me to until I was of no use to him. Leon came out of a back room with a brown duffle bag and handed it to me. The bag was full of little bags of Molly pills. I tore into one of the bags and popped two into my mouth, swallowing it down with a beer. I handed Leon three thousand dollars, that was all I had.

Leon sat on the only chair worth an ass in the room. He counting money with a cigarette hanging out the side of his lips, bobbing his head from side to side. He turned up the music with remote and the girls jumped up and started to dance. Leon signaled one of the girls by snapping his fingers then pointing at me. The teenage girl bopped her skinny body in a robotic motion towards me and plopped onto my lap. I could feel her pelvis bones poking into my thighs as she began to move back and forth trying to make my dick hard. It had been six months since I had any type of sexual activity. It wasn't by choice; I was locked up for six months for cashing bad checks.

Her Blood

The base in the music was bumping. I needed to release some tension. Leon had mentioned going to the strip club over the phone but he was sitting in the chair nodding out. My heart was beating fast, it had to be the molly kicking in. I wasn't going to make it to the club with this girl on me, my dick was getting hard. I laid my head back while the skeletal bodied girl was grinding extra slow. Her ass was getting hot, she was begging for it. Pencil eyebrow girls' ribs poked out her sides as I tried to hold onto her while she moved on top of me. I lifted her up off my lap, unzipped my pants and my big man sprang out. I guided her head down to me and began slamming into her hollow throat. There was no discussion needed, this was a part of her job. She was a whore for a living 18 or not. After I finished, Leon dropped me back at Tori's place and I told him I would hit him back in a couple days after I made his money back. When I arrived home, I crept up to Tori's' loft and stood against the wall for a moment. The aroma of lavender pierced my nose and I could hear soft snores coming from behind the curtain. She called my name and I went and laid next to her to smell her essence. After I had enough, I left out of her room before I lost control. Tori always made me lose control.

Vanessa Robinson

The guest room would have to do. I threw the bag in the closet next to some other shit Tori had stored in there. I wanted to wake Tori up and talk like old times but I didn't want her to know my situation. If Tori hit on the on the topic and started asking questions, she would see that I was lying about still owning the dealership. I wanted her to remember me as the man she used to know, the guy who saved her from her foster mother. I wanted to watch her smile at me bashfully and feel her soft hands on top of mine as she laughed. I wanted to be the man she wanted to marry and be with, before she left Boston to follow her dreams. If she knew I didn't have any money or a business and that I was selling drugs for the last few years she would've never let me stay in her home. I needed to live here rent free while I saved up some extra cash before she found everything out. I knew she had some money issues that she wasn't mentioning. I could tell just by the way her mail was stacked up. I wasn't trying to go through her mail but I accidently knocked over the pile and when I picked it up it was just bill after bill. I left a few hundred dollars on the counter next to her keys. I hope that puts a smile on her face in the morning. I'll sell the Molly at the club to get it back. I can save enough money in a month to get my own place and pay Leon back. I could see I made Tori feel nervous or like she was trying not to get close to me. I had to figure out how to vibe with her again.

Tori was the love of my life that slipped away. I wanted her to trust me again and I had to get my business back from Laura. Laura knew what it meant to me. I was the first person in family to actually make it. I could hear my uncle's voice in my head now when I first cut the ribbon at the grand opening. Uncle B stood beside smiling ear to ear "Man you made it, we're proud of you boy, we finally made it!" He gave my hand a strong shake and patted my back. I became the man of the family. Everybody came to me when they needed something and I happily gave it them. I was the man then. Laura stripped me of everything I built up in the weakest time in my life. I had kept a secret from Laura for a whole year. I was HIV positive. I had every intention on telling Laura but I was waiting until the right moment when I knew she could handle it.

One night before she came home from work, I planned to tell her my status. I cooked her favorites for dinner, bought a bouquet of roses and her peach cobbler cheesecake from Miss Mable's restaurant. I had gathered pamphlets from the clinics of the precautions we needed to take and even printed out proof to show her the risk was low since I was on the medicine. I waited at the table until the minute I heard her pulling into the driveway and met her at the door.

"Hey baby, I smell something cooking. What did you do now? You must be sorry about something!" Laura said poking her lips out for a kiss.

"You the one that smells good girl. I didn't do anything; I just wanted to feed you and treat you like the Queen you are. Come this way baby." I guided her to the table and pulled out her chair.

"Will I know you like the lines on the palm of my hand, you only cook for me when you're in trouble. You're lucky I'm starving."

"Can it just be that I want to cook for us. I'm tired of arguing about silly shit. Can we just have peace for the night." Heat was rising up my neck, sweat was itching to bust out of my pores. I slid a plate of food in front of Laura and sat down.

"I'm just busting your chops Will. I know you love to cook, but I need to tell you something serious before we eat."

"I don't want to talk business tonight; I get enough phone calls about that through the day."

Her Blood

"It's not about work, or cars..." she stopped talking and stared down at the food.

I lifted her chin until her eyes locked in mine. "Then what is it, you look nervous. What's up baby?"

"Will, I'm pregnant."

"Pregnant? How?"

"Are you serious Will?"

"That shit ain't mine, you fucking playing."

Laura banged the table knocking over her plate.

"Will we have sex more than a few times a week! How the fuck you think I am pregnant, a magic wand?" The vein in the middle of her forehead was poking out.

"Nah, a baby? We can't do this right now! It's not time Ma'. You need to fucking handle that shit !!!"

"You know what Will, you're wasting my time. FUCK YOU!!! TAKE THIS FUCKING RING AND GET OUT !!!" Laura tossed her engagement ring at me along with her glass of water. my face was drenched in water. I sat there for an hour before I went in the back room.

By midnight the diamond was back on her finger and we were covered in sweat, our legs entwined. I didn't tell her; I couldn't ruin it for her. The day she tells her fiancé she's pregnant, he tells her that life as she knows it is over. I couldn't be that guy. I was the guy who everybody needed, I had fucking made it. I couldn't take that from her.

Laura didn't mention anything that night about her status or the baby's, so I just figured she didn't have it. I went to my doctor for routine tests accordingly like always. Maybe it was gone or they made a mistake of me having it in the first place. I had been undetected for the last few months. At my last appointment the doctor ran some test just to make sure there weren't any blips happening. Doc said he would mail the results to me if they were bad. I ended up getting arrested a week later trying to cash a fraudulent check. It was the third check I was trying to cash that week and they had caught onto me. I had to serve six months for a probation violation. I called Laura every Wednesday and Friday to check on her and the baby while she worked with lawyer to get me out of jail.

Her Blood

Two months into my sentence, one Friday, I called to check on things with Laura. Around that time, she was four months pregnant. Laura was crying and upset when she answered the phone. I could hear things crashing around the apartment. Fuck! Laura had opened my mail from my doctor that read I was detectable now and the medicine he'd given me had stopped working. I knew better then to have my mail go to our place.

The venom in her voice pierced my ear drums as she screamed. I couldn't remember her usual sultry, full of spice voice that she used to coo in my ear. For days after the call I just heard her shouts "I hate you" ringing though my head, she had planted her madness inside me. The last words she said to me was that she was getting an abortion and did not want to have a child that was evil like me. I paced my cell trying to escape the mind racing images of my seed being destroyed. Laura threatened she was taking everything I had. All of the business documents were in her name, including the condo we owned. Laura had full control of everything just in case the worst happened and I couldn't move around. I knew she meant it. She outed me to the whole family, had an abortion and withdrew all the money out of my business and personal accounts.

Vanessa Robinson

Everything I worked so hard for was gone.
Some part of me knew I deserved it. I'd known for a
long time I was positive and I didn't tell her. I had
cheated on her with so many women, most of them
prostitutes, I didn't know who gave me HIV. Laura
and I didn't always use protection. We'd been
together for years and I knew she trusted me.
Many nights when we made love and she'd beg to
have my baby and I would let my seed flow inside
her and pray she would not get it. I had to, she'd
suspect something was wrong if I didn't. I was
fucked up for that, but she was more fucked up for
taking my shit.

The only person I have is Tori on my side.
When I first called Tori after I was released from
jail, I kept the conversation light to see if she would
mention that someone from back home called her
and told her about me. Tori didn't mention
anything, so it was easy to lie, everything was fine. I
told her I would fly out there but instead I hoped
on the greyhound bus. It took three and a half days
to get to California with all the stops, it gave me
time to hash out a plan. After I arrived, I took a cab
to the airport and waited for her to pick me up with
a game plan in mind. I could sell the Molly, get
enough money and then leave without a trace. As
long as Laura didn't figure out where I was while
she was on the warpath and mess it up for me,

everything would be okay. In Tori's eyes I was still the old me, even though I was getting high and still positive, I looked good to her, we still had our friendship. Tori believed in me and I wanted it to stay that way.

~Tori~

Santo Domingo

As I ran, I could hear sirens blaring loudly. Four police cars flew by me and I almost tripped off the sidewalk. My mind needed this jog, the anxiety was so high. Every loud noise had me bugging out like someone was chasing me, it just made me run harder. It was five in the morning, and the sky was still dark. Running back to my place, jogging at a slow pace I saw something. I could have sworn Mae's car was pulling off from the corner of my block. My mind had to be playing tricks on me or maybe it was a car that just looked like hers. I approached my front door there was a white paper stuck in-between the door frame and the note read "I am Sorry", signed M with a heart symbol. I guess it was her after all, she'd swung by and left me a note. I had to call her, but I wanted to do it on my own time when I was ready. I still didn't know what to say to her but I knew she wouldn't just leave this alone. Walking in the house, Will's snoring startled me, he was still asleep. I heard him come in pretty early, my silent alarm vibrated beside the bed when he opened the front door waking me up. My alarm system was set up for the hard of hearing. When I leave my house, I can turn on the alarm system but I did just to see when he would come in. I heard him creep upstairs and stand there for a minute. I called his name and he slipped through the curtain and laid on the bed behind me. He pushed his weight against my body, I could feel his meat pressing up against my cheeks, whiffs of liquor bounced of my neck. His member was brick hard. I rubbed my ass back into his groove letting my body sink into his. His big hand cupped breast his fingertips tugging at my nipple. I reached back and tried to grab his erection and will jerked back. He shot up from the bed and left the room. I didn't know why left like that. I knew I wasn't dreaming. I hope I was because it would be easier to forget.

I decided to text Dru back seeing what the good news was about. "Hi Dru, what the good news about?" she texted back almost immediately within the same minute. "You got the deal! They want a copy of your script by the end of the month!" I screamed reading the news. I texted her back "Thank you so much boo! I will come by your place later." I needed a moment to myself, after everything I been through. Finally, a breakthrough to move forward with my screen play. I didn't have anyone to tell my good news to. I wished I had a family to celebrate with. I wasn't talking to Mae and I didn't want to share with Will just yet. He seems like he is a little secretive right now and I want to find out what his situation was before I let him in. Besides celebrating with him could lead to something else I wasn't down for. I had no desire to let anyone close to me in that way for a very long time. I needed a vacation, I just needed to get away from it all and sit on a balcony with a mountain view and pour myself into my work. I don't want to deal with the reality of losing my best friend. It was still the weekend and my doctor probably wouldn't get back to me until Monday morning. I sent an email to my boss that I wouldn't be coming back in until further notice just in case I couldn't deal with the results. I emailed my travel agent to set up a vacation for me. I needed to get away to a beach or somewhere secluded with nice weather and a view of some mountains. I knew my travel agent would set me up with something serene as she always did. I took a long shower and threw on some sweats to meet up with Dru. I was in the mirror slicking down my edges, the smell of bacon crept up the stairs. Mr. creep in decided to get up and make breakfast.

I walked into the kitchen there were two plates set on the table stacked with bacon eggs and pancakes. The food looked delicious, Will cooked with chef material skills and knew his around the kitchen. I smiled at the food and watched as shirtless Will poured a tall glass of orange juice. He had very few hairs on his chest and some were sparsely spread over his stomach.

I cleared my throat loudly and said "Shirts and shoes must be worn at all times in the kitchen Sir!"

Will burst out laughing and said "Sorry Miss Lady, good morning" Will bowed his head and motioned to the food as if he was my butler "Breakfast is served Ma' Dam".

He always made me laugh, I cackled at his silliness, "Well I'm not too hungry but I'll have a few bites with you anyway, I appreciate you for thinking of me."

Will started rambling about how he wanted to stay in California a little while longer and look at places, he had another meeting with his business partner tomorrow and the two of them were working on an agreement. I could tell Will was falling in love with California the same way I did when I first moved here. The only thing that was turn off about this place was the traffic and the rent prices were sky high. There were plenty of things to do and the weather was so much better than the east coast. Will seemed happy this morning, he wasn't staring at my breast as usual and he had a plastered smile on his face. I had on fitted torn shorts and a half tank top and he never even glanced at me. I wanted to be nosey, things seemed a little mysterious about him like there was something that I didn't now. Maybe if I asked, he would give me some clues.

"So, what's in store for the week?"

He looked surprised that I asked, his eyebrows raised up.

"I might head to the inner city and explore after my meeting with my business partner, I have an old friend that's coming in town I want to meet up with."

After he said that he cleared his throat and then slurped out of his coffee cup. He stared down at his phone with his finger scrolling. It seemed like he didn't want me to ask him anything else about what he was doing or where he was going. I figured eventually whatever was going on would come out. I excused myself and said to him "See you later" he didn't take his eyes off his phone, he mouthed something but it was barely audible. I walked out the door to my car and drove off. Dru wanted to meet me at her place, she lived on the other side of town right on the beach. She owned a home with its own dock that led straight to the water, I loved visiting her place. It would be good for me to just sit on deck and watch the waves of the ocean and clear my mind. Dru and I developed a personal friendship over the last few years aside from our business relationship. I kept our friendship a secret from Mae because I didn't want her to get jealous. Some Sunday morning's when the weather was nice, I'd take a drive park my car, and have brunch on the beach. The Diner was not far from Dru's and I'd jog or walk the beach to her place just to talk and have coffee. I'd sit with her for hours talking about life and my dreams. I was more comfortable at her place than even in my own home. She had a spare room with an amazing view of the ocean. I always left something at her place in that room so I had a reason to come back. I kind of had the feeling she knew that I did that on purpose. Sometimes she would randomly text me and say "Hey your sandals miss you" with a wink emoji. It would make me bust out laughing. I think she just missed my company not the sandals. Even though she was my agent she kept her professional relationship and our friendship separate. Dru always kept it real with me, when she gave me advice about something it was always straight forward whether it was in my favor or not. I like that about her, she kept a positive outlook on life. I've known her for few years and she never had anyone in her life as far as a relationship. I knew up front when I met her that she was a lesbian but she never talked about seeing anyone. Her sexuality didn't make me uncomfortable. My truest self came out when I was in her presence. I could be completely me. Dru made me feel like her home was mine too. A while back she had given me a key to her home since I loved watching the water so much. She let me know that anytime I needed to get away I could come by her place even when she wasn't home. I used her place whenever I needed to get my head together and she always had some good Spanish food for me to munch on.

As I was passing the Diner I came up to the red light. I sat watched the water on the other side of the street. I could smell the salt water creeping into the car I decided to turn around and park at the Diner. Smith Diner was well known for its delicious pies and pastries. Mr. Smith, the owner was standing outside with his hands up on hips. He was a tall, old man with silver beard and a pot belly, dressed in overalls. The silver hair was even coming out of his ears and nose. He had a huge smile was on his face showing off his perfect set of dentures. I grabbed my satchel bag and locked up my car.

"Hey old man" I reached my arms out for a hug.

"It's been a long-time young lady, you never come see this old man anymore."

"I'm a busy woman, Mr. Smith. I'm going to get my scripts on tv!"

"Good than we need to celebrate, how about a warm piece of pie before you go."

"Screw my diet I'll take it. This diner makes the best Pies in Long Beach!"

I spoke with Mr. Smith about the good news getting my script turned into a movie, he was very happy for me and gave me two pieces of pie. He talked about seeing so many come and go in California because they couldn't make it but I hung in there. After my pie I told him I has to go meet Dru about business otherwise he would have kept me there for hours running his mouth about the locals. The first time I met him was when Dru brought me there for breakfast. Dru had breakfast there a few times a week with him spilling tea over grits and eggs. Mr. Smith mentioned she talked about me often, always telling him that I was her best client and how much she believed in me. Mr.

Smith reminded me of what it would have been like to have a grandfather. His grey eyes always carried a knowing smile like he's already lived for eternity and knew everything I was going to say before I even told him.

I carried my shoes in my hand as I walked down the beach letting my feet drown in the sand. I had turned my cell phone off so I can enjoy the sounds of the water and birds without any interruption. The sun was out warming my skin and there was a cool breeze playing peekaboo with my dress. The beach was nearly empty, there was man running with his gold retriever and family sitting on a blanket underneath an umbrella. It was a woman and a man sitting with a baby in-between them. Their lives looked so pleasant. I wish I grew up with that kind of family love. While watching them, questions started to go through my mind. Would there ever be someone that I could trust enough to have a child with or even marry? My career was heading in the right direction but my personal life turned upside down. I knew I needed to confide in someone and get another perspective of how I should handle Mae and Will. I was getting closer to Dru's house and I knew she would give me the perfect advice.

I walked up the steps onto the porch used my key to Dru's place and opened the door. I dusted my feet on the rug and headed to the spare room to wash them and put on my slippers. The aroma of Spanish food filled the house along with Dominican music. Dru was born in the Dominican Republic to an African father and Dominican Mother in the 70's. She was raised by her mother since her father left shortly after she was born. After Dru's mother died, she took her inheritance and moved to California ten years ago and bought this property. It wasn't an old house, it had four bedrooms, three bathrooms and two living rooms. Her house had a deck that ran around the whole house like a belt. It led to a back deck with a hot tub. The yard was beautiful with green grass, a rose tree and statue in the middle of a crying woman with water that flowed down her body. Dru paid to have landscapers come and design her yard for entertainment. On the patio she had a custom grill created with an iron stove on the top with a wood fire pit. The beach furniture was under the tent surrounding the fire pit. I loved her place, I told her if she was ever in the market to sell, I'd rob a bank to buy it. Her place was designed in pure serenity, you could lay in her master bed upstairs and wake up to the oceans embrace.

I walked into the kitchen and there Dru was dressed in khaki shorts and a black sports bra standing at the stove stirring a pot. The music was blasting and she was dancing her hips stirring to the beat of La Morena. Her hips swayed back and forth grooving, and she was singing the lyrics at the top of her lungs. The music belted out of the speakers and the aroma of the food filled up the house, I was in her Dominican Republic heaven. I had my phone in my hand and I started video tapping her, I knew she didn't hear me come in because of the music. It was funny watching her dance in her own world cooking and singing. She enjoyed her own company so much. I started dancing too and walked up behind her, grabbing her arm and she turned around and screamed swing a hot spatula at my head. Dru's reaction scared me and we both bumped heads, I stepped back almost falling from laughing and she grabbed me around the waist catching my fall. We were both so tickled, she pulled me upright and I rested my face into her shoulder and neck. With her arms around my waist she began dancing again and we just stood there dancing for a moment. In that moment with my eyes closed her arms I didn't want to get out of her grasp. She held the perfect rhythm guiding my hips back and forth with hers. If only my life was as smooth as this dance. Dru was the only person in my life that I could count on. I knew she had my best intentions in mind and since I've known her, she's never did anything to hurt me. After dancing

Her Blood

Dru turned down the music with the remote and I stood leaning against the counter while she finished cooking. She had chicken and rice cooking and a vegetable stir fry. The food smelled amazing and I was ready to enjoy it out on the deck with her and some wine. We made our plates and we sat down on the deck as the sun set and the waves crashed against each other.

Dru sipped and her wine we both just sat and ate; I was scared of what to say next after the romantic dancing in the kitchen. Dru spoke first.

"So how was your weekend, you look a little tired."

"It's been pretty crazy I don't know where to start."

"Start anywhere Tori" she looked serious when she said it.

a wave a sadness and guilt washed over me, I let things get out of hand with Mae. I was a little scared to tell Dru because I never talked about Mae to her. I've only spoke about the good things about my friendship with Mae to her.

"Well this weekend my good friend came over and some things happened that concerns me, it makes me sick to even talk about" She took my hand in hers and held onto it. I took a deep breath and decided to let it spill out. I told Dru everything. She sat there holding my hand listening deeply. She squeezed it when I started crying and rubbed my back. I told Dru about the trip that me and Mae took to Jamaica and how things almost went left. She didn't cut me off or speak she just listened to every word on. I told her every detail about this past Friday and even about the vile I found on the floor. When I was done, I just stopped talking and stayed quiet with my head down. The tears flowed down my face. I had said so much, even the things that I didn't want to say out loud, like having sex with another woman. Having sex with my best friend without giving sound consent. I was confused in in the moment. I couldn't look Dru in the eye, I was so ashamed of myself. Dru put her hand under my chin and lifted my head up to her eye level and the first thing she said was "It's going to be okay. I am going to help you get through this." Dru placed my hand in hers and begin to stand and brought me to my feet. She pulled me closer and wrapped her arms around me tight in a bear hug. Dru's body was warm in the nights cool breeze. Goose bumps raised up on my arms and neck. She let me go and went into the foyer and came back out quickly with a shawl and handed it to me. I wrapped up in and she said "take a walk with me." Looking up wondering what she was about to tell me I notice the sky. It was full of orange and red streaks from the sun leaving its mark. Dru walked bedside me with her hand in mine down the beach.

"Tori I want to tell you a story. I've been through a lot of things in my life. I left Santo Domingo when my mother died as I told you. Before my mother died my brother was killed by his girlfriend's ex-boyfriend. They found him with his chest stabbed up and throat slit hunched over on my mother's porch. Every morning she sat on the porch to drink her tea and watch the sunrise over the water. She found his body in a pool of blood when she opened the door. A few months after my brother was killed my mother died from a broken heart, she'd lost her son and her sunrise. The day before she died, she told me she wanted the man who killed her son to suffer. That night she died in her sleep with her Last standing Will of Testament on the nightstand. My mother left me a trust fund, her estate and my brother's share. I found out everything I needed to know about my brother's murderer. I was going to honor my mother's wishes and avenge my brother's death. When I had the opportunity to kill him, I couldn't do it. I stood in his face eye to eye and I couldn't kill him. I didn't want to end up in jail so I found a way different way to kill him. I wanted him to hurt. To suffer inside for taking away my baby brother who was my mother's pride and joy. I wanted his heart to break over and over every day. I asked a friend of mine to help me out, I knew this Italian guy that did favors for people for money. I asked him to make my brother and mother's killer suffer and gave him 100,000 dollars out of my inheritance. I was so angry, and in my mind, he took my whole family from me. Whatever that son of bitch had coming to him he deserved. Shortly after I paid the Italian guy, he called me from an unidentified number and told me to turn on the tv. I turned to the news channel and sat on the sofa. Standing in front of mansion the anchor woman spoke with a grave look on her face that a woman and child believed to be related to each other were found hanging from a tree outside the home. My stomach hit the floor and instantly I knew I had orchestrated something horrible. It was me; I was a murderer; I killed this man's family. I packed everything I had and moved out of the country within a month. I built my home here the exact same way that my mothers were built. I only took my memories and my money with me.

Dru had tears in her eyes, at this point we had stopped walking and her hands were in mine.

She had a serious look on her face. Her eyes held so much pain and regret. I pulled her close to me, I could her breath brush against my cheeks.

"Tori I am telling you this because I want you to know that I am not a perfect person. I have done some things in my life that I won't take with me to my resting place. I ran as far away from the pain I experienced and some parts of me want to face that now that I've learned to be a better person. My point of telling you this is so you can realize that you can't run from this Tori. You need to find yourself and find what Mae wants from you."

As we walked back to the house, my mind was racing. Dru made sense. I needed to know why she did this to me. Dru asked me how did I feel when I was under the influence and if Mae was into drugs. I never saw her do anything other than hit a blunt. I did go into her purse once for lipstick and she had vitamins and sleeping pills but the bottle was a generic brand from the drug store. I never opened the bottle because it wasn't my business, Dru said I should check them out. Once we were inside, we sat in her den on her long sofa drinking a glass a wine.

Vanessa Robinson

"So now that you've hit it big are you going to quit your job?" Dru asked.

"Hell yeah, I took Monday off but I'm done, I will be sending in my resignation. I'm going to keep it to myself for a while. I am not even going to tell Will I'm not working anymore. I want to see what he has going on."

"Have you talked to anybody back home?"

"Nope but I might call and see how my old friends are doing."

My phone rang, I looked at the screen and there it was a blocked number again. I let it ring out and then put my phone on vibrate.

"Are you still getting calls from Mae?"

"Yeah, I think she has been the one calling me blocked."

"Tori have you ever thought about finding your birth mother? Finding where your roots are from?"

"Yeah but I wouldn't know where to start, all I have is a picture and a name. Lee-, Lena Moore is my mother's name." An empty feeling come over me when I said her name. "Dru I always wanted to know who my mother was but my foster mother would never tell me. From what I do know she left me in Boston at 4 years old and that how I ended up getting adopted. I don't remember much about my mother but her skin was light like mine. I have is this picture that I carry with me." I showed Dru the picture.

"You look just like her but younger, very beautiful. You know I have a guy that could help you find your mother- "

"So, you must have a "guy" for everything huh?" We both burst out laughing. I moved closer to Dru on the sofa since it was getting a little drafty and I wanted some of the cozy throw she was underneath. I eased under with her, latching onto her body heat.

"Nah, I just have a lot of people that owe me some favors and he's good at what he does. I think with this shit you're going through; you need to find out where you came from. You need to know who will have your back, who your blood is." Dru had a sincere look on her face. She made me feel so safe and protected.

"You have my blessing to give your guy the picture and her name but only under one condition."

"What's that?"

"You come with me if the man finds her. If he finds anyone related to me."

"Okay I have your back". Dru pulled me close and kissed my forehead. I laid my head on her shoulder and closed my eyes. I could feel like this forever. Safe and warm. Protected. Cared for by my best friend. I could hear her heart beating through her chest. Her rhythm soothed me while her arms so tight around me. My phone vibrated on the table again breaking our embrace.

Dru looked me in the eyes "You can't run from this, answer it".

I looked down at my phone the screen said blocked. I answered and put it on speaker. "Hello".

"Is this Tori?" The girl's voice sounded unfamiliar and young.

"Who is this?"

"Never mind all that Bitch, I'm trying to help your ass! Stay away from Mae she is dangerous." The call ended before I could get a word out and I couldn't call back because the number was blocked. Dru and I both looked at each other in dismay and confusion. I had no idea what to say.

"Who the hell was that?"

"I don't know. I've never received a call like this before." I started to feel panic bubbling inside of me, I was a boiling pot ready to spill over. My mind wandered to the mysterious vile I gave my doctor. I couldn't breath again.

Dru put her arm around me. "Stay here with me tonight."

I shook my head up and down because I couldn't speak. There was no way I could drive home with this shit on mind. I would probably end up on the side of the road crashed into a tree. I poured another glass of wine and gulped it down.

Dru rubbed my back. "It's going to be alright we're going to get to the bottom of this."

~Taylor~
I know what you did

Mae's ass thought she was slick. This bitch is off her meds and acting crazy again. I rummaged through her purse while she was in the bathroom. Some doctor lady called here looking for her last week. Since I was her emergency contact, she wanted to notify me that Mae had been MIA from her therapy appointments and not returning any of her phone calls. I told the lady I could try to help her get back on track if I ran into her but I couldn't guarantee it. I didn't see any medicine bottles in her bag or prescription receipts. I saw daddy's knife in there and it reminded me of those days when he was bent down in hood of the car on the weekends. I was the first thing I would see it clipped onto his back pocket when I asked him for change to buy candy. After he died on a fishing trip with Mae, she mysteriously had it. I took her phone out of her purse and to my surprise it was unlocked. Mae was the most secretive person I knew she had locks on everything, she was definitely off. Swiping through her phone I didn't see any calls back to the doctor, she rejected them all. There were hundreds of calls to somebody in her phone named Tori. If I didn't know any better this chick fucked her man or Mae was stalking somebody again heavy. There was a text from the Tori chick that read "LEAVE ME ALONE !!!", In all caps but no other messages. I knew Mae was unpredictable off her medication and she could hurt somebody. I called the Tori girls number to give a warning. I wasn't trying to start no shit but this girl needed to be aware of who she was dealing with. The girl that answered after a few rings, she had an east coast accent when she said Hello. I said what I had to say and hung up. I didn't have time to explain. I heard Mae's heels sashaying out the bathroom. I ran back into the kitchen and threw her phone back in her purse.

Vanessa Robinson

"Where the hell you been at Mae? I know you haven't been taking your medication."

"I don't need medication and you need to know shit about my life. Taylor mind your business."

"Mae you come around me every couple of months looking for money and then I don't see you after that. Between you and mama begging for the money daddy left me, I won't have any left by the end of the year!"

"Bitch you the one drinking it up, laid up here in this nice house. George didn't leave me a damn dime and I'm the oldest. I should have the money not you!" Mae banged her hand on the table knocking over my wine.

Here we go again, I wasn't daddy's favorite girl, but he knew I was the responsible one and he left me the money. Mae always wanted to cry and argue about why he left it to me because I was the younger one. Maybe if this bitch wasn't so psychotic, she would have it. She tried to put me on a guilt trip every time she brought her ass over here. Everyone in the family knew she was unstable and she took right after mommy. It was a rumor that after Mae was born Mama started doing drugs really bad and Mae was living all over the place until foster care took her. Mae's life was hard for those two years in the system. They say Mama used to sleep with men for money in the streets while she was getting high.

For a few years she disappeared and nobody could find her. It was rumor she had a baby while addicted to drugs. Some old heads say they seen her cracked out pregnant, during that time she was missing. They said once she had it, she sold the baby for money to get high. I once asked her about the rumor but she never gave me a clear answer. Her mouth would twist up like she couldn't get the words out, then she would change the subject. Trying to get information out of her is too much work picking through the lies for the truth. I don't have time for the bullshit. When Lena gets on the topic of the past she will go on and on about a bunch of nothing and then tell me to get out her face. Her favorite line is "Stay out of grown folks' business." We never had a good relationship. Back then when mama resurfaced from being MIA, she was big and pregnant with me. Daddy tried to make an honest woman out of her and persuaded her to get married. George convinced mama to get Mae out of foster care and they moved here to San Diego. It's still a mystery as to whether she had a baby or not. I know better though; I believe she did have a child and just too embarrassed to say because she was on drugs.

Growing up with Mae she was so different than me, she was nearly fully developed by the age of ten. Mae and daddy always went on fishing trips and when she would come home, she acted different. Mae would act out in school and runaway for days at a time. Nobody where she went or what she was doing when she was missing. Mama took her to the doctor and they told her that she had loss touch of reality. It was in and out for her, one minute she would be calm and normal the next out of control. The doctors gave her psychiatry medication to take once a day. They made her into a zombie but if she didn't take them every day, she would be out of control again before the weeks end. As Mae became older her "condition" as I called it seemed to get worse, she would stop taking her medication for months at a time and lose control of her life. Everything that went wrong in her life she blamed daddy. She accused daddy of molesting her for years, but didn't say anything until after he died.

The last time they went on a trip together he never came home and may couldn't talk for weeks. It's like she was a complete zombie. No one knew the truth about what happened to her or him. They found his body in the water a month later

Vanessa Robinson

but it was in parts. Some of his body parts
were missing and the police speculated that
he had fallen out of the boat and drowned
and the fish fed off him. Mae was found
drifting in the boat, in the middle of the
ocean by herself, my father gone. Mae never
spoke about that day. Mama took her to
therapist after therapist and she wouldn't
open her mouth. I wasn't stupid though, I
know Mae did something to daddy. Daddy
always had his knife tucked in his back
pocket wherever he went. How did Mae
come back with it? She carries it everywhere
in her purse just like he did in her pocket. It's
like she's bringing him with her. I know for a
fact my daddy would have died with his knife
in his pocket. Mae would never tell. I will get
it out of her one day. I miss daddy, she took
him away from me, I will always hate Mae
for that.

I gulped down my third glass of wine
waiting for Mae to leave. Mae stood on the
other side of the counter glaring at me. Her
nails tapping on the granite counter top
waiting for me to fill her hand with some

money. Her glare was so evil and ugly. She didn't like me and I knew it. I didn't want anything to do with her but I thought I had too. My sister was so beautiful on the outside like a model but on the inside, she was rotten to her core. Mae was good at faking it with other people, she didn't care about anyone but herself and what she wanted.

"Mae, I have one thousand dollars for you, you need to figure out what you going to do because I don't have any more money to give you." I handed her the money and she snatched it out of my hand, scratching my arm.

"Don't snatch from me you demon ass bitch" I wanted to punch her but I knew I couldn't reach across the counter fast enough.

"Fuck you bitch, I know there is more money somewhere! You keep hiding it from me Taylor, some sister you are. You would rather see me starve them help me out a little bit."

"That's nonsense, I've given you thousands of dollars this year and its never enough. Just get a job, I can't support you anymore. I'm tired."

"Then take a nap. You have it to give, you just don't want to and that makes you a bloodless bitch." Mae snatched up her purse and stomped to the front door. Heels jarring into the hardwood floor.

"You're not entitled to my inheritance Mae. The only thing I have for you from this point on is advice bitch, seek help! Stay the fuck away from me!"

"No worries, I won't be back. I will never ask you for anything else."

"Please don't! I don't need this type of energy, you're draining me."

"Well now you can light your little sage and candles, and pray I don't come back and fuck you up Taylor!" Mae walked out the door, she kicked over the plants on the steps and sped off fucking up the grass.

I'm done with her. I'm sick of her and mama begging me for money. Mama couldn't stay clean more than a few hours and she came to the house for money every week and it wasn't small amounts. I did feel bad for her because daddy didn't leave her a dime either because he knew of her past drug habit. Daddy knew if anything ever happened to him, she would be right back on drugs because she couldn't handle life without him. After Mae pulled off, I slammed my door nearly knocking it off the hinges and dialed my relator. I needed to move and get the hell up out of here.

~Tori~

Vile Shit

Last night I slept next to Dru on the sofa. It was the best sleep I've had in a long time, even though I didn't have much space to spread out. Throughout the night I could feel her holding me. Her arms were strong and she had them wrapped around my waist tightly when I woke up. I grabbed my phone off the coffee table and there was a missed call from my Doctor. I jumped up and ran to the porch to call her back. Dru followed behind shortly with a cup of coffee for each of us. I just sat there for a few minutes praying; I was scared of the results she would give me. My heart was beating fast but I knew I needed to call my doctor back to find out what I had taken. I pressed send with phone on speaker, she answered immediately and asked if I was sitting down.

"Are you with you're the friend who you suspect drugged you?"

"No." I'm with someone I can trust." My breathing was getting fast.

"So, what was in it the little vile? What are my blood results?" I said in a haste.

"Well first Tori I need you to calm down before you give yourself a heart attack. Normally I give these results in office but I wanted you to know as soon as possible just in case you're in danger. In the vile and in your blood, we found the same substance called Scopolamine."

"What the hell is that?" I was dumbfounded by the information she was giving me.

"It's a drug used to make a person submissive or forget what's happening to them. Your body had above high levels of it. It's comes in a powder form and it can quickly dissolve into a drink, I'm assuming that's how it entered your system."

My mouth was just hanging open I couldn't even speak how could my best friend do such a thing to me.

The Doctor continued, "It originated in Colombia and comes from plants, used in the early nineteen hundred's for anesthesia or for pain. Now a days it's used as a date rape drug. Whomever gave you this drug, was trying to get you to be submissive and not remember the events of the night. Do you remember anything from Thursday night?"

"Yes, I do, I remember almost everything" It was still foggy but I almost had a perfect recap.

"Tori for you to have any memory at all you are truly lucky. The drug when given in high doses can leave you physically and mentally powerless for twenty-four hours and causes amnesia. When its ingested it makes a person have hallucinations, blurred vision, confusion and lots of other side effects. All of that is even more powerful when combined with alcohol. I think you should press charges this is a serious crime. The person who gave you this drug did not have good intentions."

"Doctor that will be something I have to think about, thank you. Is there anything else I should know?"

"Yes, we did find a small trace of alcohol, ecstasy and marijuana as well but that's it. I will have to make a report to my superiors, but I will not alert law enforcement, that's up to you. Please take care of yourself."

I just sat there in dismay. I've never knowingly did ecstasy in my life. I did smoke weed here and there but most of the times it was with

Mae and never a stranger. I hung up the phone. Dru was sitting there with a look of shock on her face, holding her breath.

"Tori how well do you know Mae? What's her background?" Dru asked looking me dead in my eyes.

"I don't know, I learned just bits and pieces over time, she never gave me the full story of her life. When we hang, we just focus more on the now rather than the past."

After the words passed my lips, they sounded silly playing it back in my head. How could I not know vital information about her past?

"Mae told me she grew up in San Diego, California and she told me she was an only child. Her parents passed away when she was younger and then she was adopted."

I kind of stopped learning information at adoption. After I told her I was a foster child she came out to me that she was too, that is one way we bonded with each other. I kind of had a knowing of what her life may have been like from my own experiences. I never pressed for any details because I didn't want to open up any childhood wounds and I didn't want her digging into mine. I don't know too much more."

We both sat there for a minute just staring into space. Dru was dancing on the line of violating my privacy. I wanted to kick her ass but what good would that do. More than anything I wanted to know who I was dealing with. This wasn't just her getting me drunk trying to fuck around, she was playing with my life. My mind kept swirling with what-if questions and what type of state-of-mind she was in to get the idea to drug me with an ancient drug.

Dru plopped her mug on the table busting me out of my thoughts.

"I'll get my guy to look into her, I'll text him the information you do know about her. He might be able to come up with something. I just need important stuff from you like her birthday, full name and where she lives." I gave it to her, not even knowing if that shit was for real.

Dru went into the house to reach out to her friend. I sat in the chair feeling like the world was closing in on me. I was son an emotional rollercoaster right at the top before it goes down that long slope. My stomach was turning in knots. I wanted to give her the benefit of doubt, maybe she thought the drug was something else, maybe she was sold the wrong stuff. Could this have been a prank gone wrong? Why the ecstasy? Was Mae in love with me? Was she even adopted like she said? I knew nothing about my best friend when shit hit the fan. My head started pounding with a migraine. I was going to have to do my own digging.

~Lena~

Don't mind the man,
Mind the money

My eyes watched the money on the corner of the mattress as my body rocked back and forth on top of it. The money didn't move an inch, just five more minutes is all he needs and then I can go see daddy. I like the way James do me, he does it better, he doesn't drip no sweat on me. James like to say my name instead of calling me "hoe or slut" like this one. James whispers things in my ear with his raspy voice like "Give me this tired old' pussy gal" that's when I know James is high as a kite. If Taylor wouldn't have disappeared into thin air, I could have gotten some money from her and I wouldn't have to sell it. If I bother her enough, I know she will call me back. I have to keep leaving them messages so she can feel bad for keeping my late husband money from me.

This sure ain't my dead husband George on top of me but it feels like it. Just two more minutes on this mattress, he's fucking me like he's in hurry, I think he's on his lunch break. The sweat dripping on down my neck now but he ain't barely moving. Poor thang ain't bigger than my pinky finger wiggling inside me, feeling slimy trying to catch my depth. Mr. Lunchbreak grunted in my ear and his face came down between my shoulder. "Get off me, it cost extra for that! You nasty dog!" I grabbed my forty dollars off the mattress. James met me at the back-yard door and snatched the money out my hand. I could tell was mad the way he back leaning off his bad leg like he was ready to jump on me.

"Come on gal, what you were doing back there making love!" he yelled. His lips were turned up with the white stuff on the sides, I knew he started smoking without me. He was probably jealous lunch break said he'd be back tomorrow same time.

James leaned back on the wall eyeing the younger man until he disappeared. James wasn't the pimp he used to be when I met him in the 80's but he kept me solid. James only had me left now, once the money dried up, his friends disappeared. I didn't like what I had to do but at least I was able to get us some money to live off. I walked behind James into the house dodging the trash on the floor and the roaches ready to jump off the wall. It was old food, liquor bottles, dried up throw up, and piles of shit all over the place since the plumbing ain't working. This was our house for now, James promised If I keep working hard, we can save up for better. I keep seeing him do is buy more crack for us to get high. I can't remember the last time we looked for new place to live. It's not so bad here, besides I like nobody not being able to find me. I once had a nice place with George. I fixed up the house real nice with decorations and furniture. The grass in the yard was green, not like this yard that full of rusty old tires, condoms and trash. My yard with George had furniture in it and a pool for the girls. I would invite the other mothers over with their kids and they would tell how nice my house was. They would say Lena you living the life girl, I hope I find a husband like yours. George would buy me nice things like pearls and designer skirts with flowers hand sewed on it. George was a good man who took good care of me. Everybody said I was lucky he picked me to be his wife.

My momma used look down underneath her glasses and say to me "Don't mind the man, mind the money baby."

I think she taught me right, he made sure we had everything. He wanted us to be the perfect family. He always wanted a son and when I had Mae in 1979, he made me name her after his daddy, Maze. I'll never forget I was laying in the hospital bed admiring my baby's hair.

"I want to name her after my daddy" George said.

"George, Maze is not fit for a girl, let's just take out the "Z" and call her Mae. We went back and forth for a while but then he finally settled on the name Mae. It seemed like he loved Mae more than me at times, but I didn't mind because I wanted him to protect her.

George was a real hard-working man, when he started driving trucks across country, that's when things took a bad turn for bad for me. He would be gone months at a time driving them trucks and I ain't have nobody to love me. I had a whole baby and I couldn't stop crying and the baby too. George was gone working, so I started hanging with my neighbor girlfriend to get a break. My neighbor gave me a little something to help the depression, I started feeling happier and hanging out more. That's around the time I met James he was pimping girls but I didn't want no parts of it. When George was gone for months, my neighbor would watch the baby and James would take me on the town and spend his money. We would be eating, drinking and smoking too. When George would come home, I would put my pretty skirts back on and stay in the house, to keep George from find out I was cheating. He would only come home for a week and then be back on the road for months. George kept saying he saving so we can move west to California but I didn't care. I liked Boston and I wanted to stay close to James. We called James "Daddy" since he had the girls and the money. I knew he was married and had them girls but he said he loved only me.

In 1984 I found out I was pregnant by James. George had been gone so long I didn't know what to do. He never would make love to me when he came home so I knew it had to be James baby. It must have happened one of them nights we were turning out and getting high.

I started at James sitting on the floor sucking on the pipe like it was going to disappear. He was looking run down, he barely had hair on his head now. His cheeks are sunken on the side like a fish and his eyes wide. He used so be so handsome and his hands so pretty cause' he never worked a day in his life. When I started to look pregnant, one day James came and picked me up and in brand new Cadillac. I dropped Mae off at the neighbors and we went for a long ride. I didn't go back home for almost 2 years; I was in love. I was James's bottom bitch now; I did everything for him. James had left his wife and he kept me high the whole time I was pregnant. When the baby came out, she wouldn't stop crying until we lit the pipe up and blew smoke in her face. James said he would make sure he would take her to a safe place because we couldn't keep her on the streets. I just wanted to get high at the time, I didn't care where he took her. The was baby was so tiny I didn't think she would make it through the week. I couldn't let George find out I had a baby on him. Nobody knew where I was or what I was doing, they just knew I was gone. James took the baby away and when he came back, he had a big brown paper bag full of money. We were high for every day for months like zombies. All my hair fell out and I started turning tricks when the money ran out. One night I was working the streets for James standing on my corner waiting for a trick. A real shiny car with dark windows pulled up and sat there for a minute. I walked up and the window cracked open, a man's voice said "Get in foxy." I just knew I hit the jack pot just by the way the car was gleaming in the dark, it was so clean and looked like money. I sat on suede seats in the passenger side and shut the door. When I looked up, low and behold my wig shifted back in shock, it was George. That was the time he almost killed me and made me come back home.

Her Blood

Vanessa Robinson

~Will~

A Hole in the Wall

Tori didn't come home last night, she had to be at some niggas house. I didn't recall her telling me that she had a man but it must be somebody. I reached out to her and left a text but I didn't get a response. She was acting kind of funny yesterday like she was scared the Feds were going to come to the door. Tori doesn't know I have the pills in my room so I don't know why she was so paranoid. I wanted her to think of me was "I'm that guy." Riding dirty wasn't my way of staying low key but I didn't have a choice. I needed to sell these pills and get money fast. I was headed to the spice club where I heard it gets crowded with all ages and the drugs are flowing. I drove by the club and the line from the entrance was down the block. The reggae music was blasting off the rooftop. I could see mostly girls in line with barely any clothes on. I was ready to hear some good music and get some pussy after I made this money. I pulled in the parking lot and stashed the pills in my sneakers. I intentionally bought some Jordan's two sizes bigger so I'd have enough room to stash them. When this batch is gone, I'm going to come back to the car and reup and sell the rest.

When I walked in the club it was already packed and people were still coming in. The club was dark, it gave me an old school feeling with the DJ upstairs watching people jam to the music. There was a spotlight in the middle of the ceiling going around and around grazing people faces. The air was tight from the weed smoke coming out of the dark corners. I couldn't walk a few feet without going through a cloud of smoke. To see how the females looked I had squint through the darkness or wait until the spot light hit them, but even that was dim. I posted up in the corner for an hour to watch the crowd build and to see who was in need. As time pushed on, I was serving them left and right. I noticed that standing closer to the entrance of the bathroom brought me more business. I would stop the guys and ask them if they need something and if they nodded, I'd follow them into the bathroom and make the exchange. I stopped the girls by saying "Hey beautiful you want some candy?" and if they were tipsy enough when they stopped, I'd open up the palm of hand and show her the pill. It was getting close to the club closing and I only had a few pills left after running back to the car a few times. I noticed a caramel skin sexy girl watching me from the distance. I almost thought it was Tori from afar. The way she was shaped and her hair was the same, dark and curly. She started coming towards me with a playful look on her face. The girl walked with so much sass, her ass switching side to side. She came so close to me I could smell the scent of her perfume. Her breath smelled like vodka and weed when she parted her lips. She had a joint in her hand between her long nails, she put her free arm around my neck and began wining her pussy on me. It was damp between her legs as she grinded. The look in her brown eyes was magnetic, I couldn't look away. Damn this girl reminded me of Tori they even had the same birthmark on their faces. She was grinding on me hard, I turned her around and placed her ass on me and she took control, bending over making circles with her ass on my pelvis. I matched her grind and we danced a whole song in that position. Damn she was sexy. Her waist was so small and I could tell she worked out because her legs were thick and toned. She wore a tiny top that tied around her waist like a belly dancer. Little beads of sweat dripping trailing down to her ass.

The music changed and she guided me towards the back corner of the club where it was dark and the spotlight couldn't reach. I followed looking around, the back wall was full of people lined up. I couldn't tell if the people were dancing or fucking. The sexual tension was heavy and my dick was hard from her ass grinding on me and watching couples dance like they were in heat. I had popped a pill earlier to prove to a girl it wasn't going to kill her so she could buy it. I was feeling that now. I wanted to pull this girl by her hair and pull her panties to the side right here. She had on a long flowy type skirt like she was straight from the islands. She pushed me up against the back wall and stood in front of me pressing her body up against mine. I put my face in-between her neck and licked behind her ear. Damn even her sweat tasted good. She put her hand on my hard dick and started caressing it. I stared into her eyes trying to see what her angle was. Her facial expression was dark, she had a sly grin spread over her red lips, she knew she succeed at turning me on. I could tell she was high or drunk or something. I had caught a contact when I first walked in from the smoke in the air. I had four shots given to me from a few people I sold to, to thank me for looking out. The chicks in here were basic, something about her was different though. From the time she walked over to me she had not spoken so finally I asked her name.

"What's your name baby?" pulling her closer to me so I could hear.

"Does it matter?" she slurred.

"Yeah, so I can say it while you riding what you grabbing." She laughed a little when I said that and she started unzipping my pants.

"My name is Taylor, and who said I'll be riding anything?" she smirked.

I was molding her plump ass in my hands and as we stood there, swaying back and forth, waiting on each other to make the next move. She fumbled around a little to get under my boxers and then her bare hands were wrapped around my piece. She started pumping it up and down, I tried to hold onto my sanity. I never met a woman that was so nasty in the club, she was the perfect stranger. She was stroking it just right... up and down... side to side. Damn she was getting it ready. I leaned in to kiss her lips and she pulled her head back. She whispered in my ear, "Not here."

The crowd around us thickened up. I could see people behind her bunched up their bodies gyrating in motion with the music.

"Where" I said, staring straight into her eyes. She backed up a few feet from me and signaled her hand in a stay motion for me not to move. She was gone for a few minutes. I stood there against the wall observing the crowd with my dick at attention.

Her Blood

When she came back around the corner, she was walking a little funny but smiling.

Taylor leaned into me with her breast resting on my chest. The lights flickered off and on for two seconds to signify last call. Suddenly she said "Never mind" and turned around in a hurry to leave. I quickly grabbed her by the waist pulling her backside towards to me and lifted up her skirt. She didn't have on any panties, I put my fingers inside her wetness. She was playing games with me. Taylor struggled to get out of my grasp but I was much stronger. I held her with my right arm around her waist and her free arm pinned underneath mine. I turned both of us around with her now facing the wall, the side of her face pushed up to it. The crowd was going wild over an old reggae song that came on. They were grinding, jumping up, waving bandannas, pressed up against the wall and sweating just as we appeared to be. I could hear her screaming get off me through the music. I grabbed my dick and started pushing into her bare ass. I did her just the way she did me when she first waltzed over to me. I went deep inside her to the rhythm of the song. She kept pushing back on me trying to get me off of her. I pushed her harder into the wall. Her face against it, lips curled up with saliva coming down. I tasted her sweat again. She was more intoxicating than the shots I had. "I whispered in her ear; you like this dance baby? You like this whine?" I was out of breath. She tried to scream but it came out as a hoarse moan. I tried to cover her mouth but she bit my thumb with all her might. Pulling back my bloody hand in pain, out came her sharp screams, they vibrated into the wall with the music. The vibrations went through me too and I let go inside of her. I collapsed onto her body up against the wall as sweat dripped down my face. I pulled my jeans up and walked out of the club. When I looked back, she had slid down the wall and no one noticed. The crowd probably thought she was drunk and passed out with her skirt up. Her lips had blood on it from biting my thumb. I walked as fast as I could to the parking lot, not looking back again. I swallowed the last pill I had in my pocket. I let it dissolve in my mouth, the settling feeling started in my jaw then to arms and my head. I was in control again. I lost it in there. Shit. I waited outside the club watching to see if she would come out the door, but she never came out. Maybe she disappeared into the crowd and I missed her. I wanted to apologize if I was too rough, I was caught up in the moment. I drove to Leon's, I was too wired up to go to sleep and at his house it was always a party. I hoped those girls were there from the last time.

Her Blood

Vanessa Robinson

~Taylor~
Smoke in the Spotlight

White, that's all I could see. I didn't know if I was dead or alive. As I struggled to open my eyes, I could see the image of a man leaning down on me shining a flashlight into my face. He kept asking me if I was okay. I heard another voice in the back scream. The scream, it was like a car screeching sound that pierced into my head like knife. Something bad must of happen to me. My heart was beating out of my chest. I didn't know where I was. Opening my eyes looking down, why was I half naked? The last thing I could clearly remember was earlier in the day. I remember meeting with Mae, she had called me and asked if she could apologize. She said that she was back on her medicine and wanted to meet for drinks. I was hesitant to meet with her because I didn't have any proof that she was back on her medication. I wanted to make sure she would be civil and she sounded sincere on the phone. I met with her at a popular bar & grill downtown and we talked over dinner. Mae apologized for a lot of things she had done to me over the years. She even apologized for teasing me when I was little and abusing me. She apologized for treating me like an outsider of the family because she wanted both of our parent's attention to herself. Mama was barely there anymore but she said she wanted to have a better family relationship. She showed me her medicine bottle and the look in her eyes was different. It seemed like she was honest with her feelings and wanting my forgiveness.

After dinner she suggested that we go out on the town and bond with each other. I was skeptical at first since this isn't the first time, she did this act. Mae did this before coming to me and trying to make up and say sorry just to get money. This time though she didn't ask for anything but friendship so I decided to give her a second chance. I have to admit I was excited because Mae and I never did those sisterly things together because she was too controlling and we didn't get along. Now that she agreed to turn over a new leaf, I was open to get to know this new side of my sister and have a good time with her. She told me she had a "friend of a friend" for me and that he wanted to meet at the reggae club. It had been a while since I been out. R&B music was more my thing but it wouldn't hurt to try something new and besides Mae knew I was looking for a man. Mae said she brought clothes for us to wear out. We both dressed in semi alike wearing long flowing skirts and a crop top that wrapped around the waist and tied in the back. I booked a hotel room near the club in case I was too tipsy to drive home. The hotel room created a distance between Mae and my home. I didn't want Mae to think she was all the way back in with me. My house was peaceful and I wanted to keep it that way. We drank wine on the balcony and talked about fun times when we were younger. I started to feel buzzed faster than usual and suggested we go to the club to meet the friend she had for me. I wanted to get this over with before I was too intoxicated to see. It had been years since I had a guy friend or been on a date. I was nervous as hell about meeting someone new. Mae kept pouring me glasses of wine to ease my nerves. She had also mentioned her guy friend would meet us there too so it would be like a double date. We hit the dance floor as soon we walked in the club, my feet were tingling and my ass didn't miss a beat. The room was spinning and the music was pumping. I thought I was on top of the world. Mae lit a joint and passed it to me and things get foggy from there. I remember dancing. I remember being in the bathroom with the green walls. I remember staring down at the broken tiles on the floor while I squatted over the toilet peeing. I remember sneezing from the smoke burning my nose. I remember counting the exit signs throughout the club, in a case a fire broke out. Then I remember being pinned against the wall being raped. Where the fuck was my sister now. The last I saw my sister she was dancing beside me pointing to the guy I was supposed to meet. I remember the throw up coming up to my throat and excusing myself to the bathroom. I stood at the sink drinking from the faucet as if it was the last drop of water on earth. My throat was so dry and my head was spinning out of control. Other women were walking by me looking me up and down, shaking their heads in disgust. I remember the sound of their heels clicking by. They sounded like hammering broken glass into the floor. About ten minutes later Mae came in and told me she was ready to go because her dude canceled. Mae said I should at least say "Hi" to her friend and exchange numbers, it would be rude not to. I straightened my skirt up a bit and tired my best to walk straight. When I reached the strange awkward fine man on the back wall it was pitch dark. I smiled and leaned in so he could hear me, before I could say anything, I wobbled from side to side. I put my hand on his muscular shoulder to keep from falling and nearly fell into his arms. The lights came on with a blast and I freaked out and said forget it. This guy just took over me and pinned me to the wall. I never been so scared in my life. No one could hear me screaming. He covered my mouth and I bit deep into his flesh but that didn't work. He just pushed harder into me over and over like a monster and then left me for dead.

Sitting in the ambulance, the paramedic asked me If I wanted to go the hospital since I had blood on my skirt and mouth. I shook my head up and down. I couldn't even talk I was so ashamed. As they wheeled me into the emergency room it reeked of sickness and pain. A lady laid out in the bed with her eyes closed. That could have been me there dead. How could I be so stupid. I felt horrible, I ached all over, especially in the inside parts. Where the hell was my big sister at and why would she leave me at a club alone under the influence? My body was drained and I know for sure I was raped every muscle was sore. I questioned myself. Did I fight hard enough? I know how to fight; I am a fighter. Sitting there in silence for over an hour waiting on the doctor my mind raced. I wracked my brain trying to remember details. I kept reliving bits and pieces of the night over and over. Asking myself questions and answering them. The doctor came back in the room and did a rape kit on me and a series of test for any sexually transmitted diseases. After the examination, humiliation had set in. The way the nurse's eyes peered into me; she was judging me. She pulled her blue gloves out of the box on the wall and slapped them open into the air, the noise frightened me. She stood at the end of the bed staring at me with her practiced empathy face, silently shaming me. How could I let this happen to me? Why did I get so drunk? Did I say no? I don't remember saying no. Tears flooded me from the inside out.

When they released me from the hospital, I caught a taxi home. I ran the shower and stepped in with the hospital scrubs still on. I peeled off my clothes and sat on the tub floor. I stayed there until the water was ice cold crying and scrubbing the shame off me. That man was a sick fuck. Emotions were a runaway train at one time. Humiliation, rage thicker than a brick. Pain boiled inside me. I prayed he did not give me any diseases. If he did, I wanted to shed his blood. I'm going to find this man but first I have to find Mae. That bitch let him rape me. I hate her! She encouraged me to go over to him knowing that I was drunk. She left me there like a piece of trash. I can only blame myself for falling for her lies again. She has to have something to do with this. Maybe he thought I was her since we were both dressed alike. When I get better, I'm going to find out what Mae did and I am going to find this man too. I sat at my desk with a pillow underneath my butt since it was sore and opened up my laptop. I knew Mae's phone account password; I logged into her account online and begin to write down the number of the girl I gave the warning to. If anybody knew anything it had to be her. It just had to be, I wanted revenge. Fuck Family, Fuck Mae! Her blood ain't shit.

Her Blood

Vanessa Robinson

~Mae~

Gone Fishing

Three days has passed and still haven't heard from Tori. I followed the GPS location of her car and found it parked on the board walk in front of an old broken-down diner. It didn't look like too many people would want to eat here. I could smell the roach powder at the door. She sure wasn't in there and the old man at the counter acted like he didn't know who I was talking about. He kept saying. "You sure you have the right place young lady?" with a deep puzzled look on his face.

I had a picture on my phone and showed it to him and he asked if It was a relative, I said "No." I knew she had to be close. I sat in the Diner looking at the old-celebrity-has-been photos on the wall. Looked like the old man put his wife on display. All the photos were in a brownish black and white color, the woman was smiling in the frames like she won a prize. I sat there feeling defeated with my head down staring at my phone. I looked half way up and the old man was standing at the edge of the table looking at me with a smile plastered on his face.

Her Blood

"What you want old man?" I didn't have time for him questioning me about the picture I showed him.

"Now don't blow your dust lady, I just came over to offer you a piece of pie. We make the finest pie on the beach."

I noticed he had the pie in his hand. He sat the small plate of pie on the table and came around to sit down. His old knees cracked when his bottom hit the bench.

"What you need to find this young lady in the picture for? Is she in trouble?" He looked concerned like he might just know who Tori was. I wanted to correct his English but you can't teach an old dog new tricks.

"No, she's not in trouble but she's my friend and I need to get in touch with her, I don't know where she is and her car is outside."

After I said that his long thick eyebrows raised. He cleared his throat and just sat there in silence. His fingers tapped the counter to the Frank Sinatra music playing in the background.

"Look, I have some customers to tend to. You enjoy your pie and I hope you find your friend." He limped away in a hurry to greet the new people who walked in.

I didn't want to talk to him about anything else anyway. His eyebrows gave me the hint he knew her when I mentioned the car. He had to know, it's been sitting there for a day or two. I decided to go by her house again to see if her friend Will was home. I didn't want him to know exactly who I was. I never met him before and when Tori and I do make up I want her to introduce me as her friend. I don't want Will to know anything about the other night. I swung by my place to change clothes. I put a tight blue dress and spike heels. I put on a blonde straight wig, since my real hair was curly and black. I put on dark purple lipstick and opened the top of the dress so my cleavage can show. Before I walked out of the house, I grabbed a box of sample lotions given to me by my hairdresser.

Turning the corner of Tori's place, it was the middle of the afternoon, none of her neighbors were home. I could hear the music pumping from inside of the house as I pulled in the driveway. I guess her friend Will was having a grand time while Tori was away. It wasn't like her to blast rap music in the middle of the day, she was more on the softer side and listened to Neo Soul and Jazz type of music. I stood at the door trying to hear voices but the music was too loud. I pounded on the door and kicked it a few times. The door swung open and it threw me for a surprise. Will was super fine. He stood in the doorway shirtless starting back at me like I disrespected him. His muscles looked like they were carved onto his body. He was a smooth buttery dark chocolate color. I could imagine if I licked him, he would melt in my mouth. He had a low cut and his fade looked airbrushed on it was so fly.

"Hi, I'm sorry to interrupt you. I came by to deliver theses lotions for Tori is she home?" I said.

"Nah, she not home today but I can take it for her." He reached out his hand to grab the box but I snatched it back playfully.

"And you are?" I asked swinging my hair back.

"I'm her friend Will, is it lotion you have? The way you snatched it back you sure it ain't gold?" he laughed.

"Well I wouldn't want you to use her lotion for yourself this is expensive", I glanced down at the large poke coming through his grey sweatpants and smiled. He saw me smile and looked down too.

"Nah I don't use lotion I have better things for that. Would you like to come in?" He opened the door wider and motioned for me to step in. I stepped inside and sat the box on the table.

"Do you know when she might be coming back?"

"Look I don't her schedule I suggest you call her, what's your name again?"

"Kim, I said smirking. There's no way I could give him my real name, and my pussy was starting to feel wet, but I couldn't take those chances if Tori showed up. After all this was her house. I needed to hurry up and get the information that I needed. I needed to know where she was.

"That's a nice dress Kim, listen I'm going to a reggae spot tonight called Spice, it would be nice of you to come join me." Was he asking me out? His game was so weak.

"I didn't strike you for the reggae type of guy with the rap music playing, but yeah, I'll stop in. Let Tori know I stopped by." I grabbed my purse and walked out the house, Will followed.

"Can I get your number though?" he was so close to me I could smell the weed on his breath.

Her Blood

"Nope, you will see me there" I said teasingly.

I let the short dress ride up my thighs. I took out my compact mirror and saw Will watching my ass all the way to my car. He retreated back into the house when my car was out of sight. I ripped off my Wig and threw it in the back seat. Why the fuck didn't he know where she was.

Taylor was calling my phone back to back; I hope she wasn't calling about taking the medicine again. That shit made me into zombie, I couldn't sleep or eat on it. Besides there was nothing wrong with me. I was perfectly fine without it and I was more ambitious without it. I was going after what I wanted. Taylor made me out to be some money hungry angry person trying to ruin the family. She made the whole family think I was a crazy liar. She knew what daddy was doing to me every night. She would be sleeping in other bed and sometimes she would wake up and see daddy lying next me. George would pretend like he was asleep or reading a bedtime story to me. As soon as she fell back asleep, he would be right back on top of me. Every time he took me on a fishing trip, we didn't catch no fish. I was the fish. George would rape me even when we would go out on the water. He would make me go naked and the only thing he wore was his fishing pants with his pocket knife. On the boat he would talk about how he much he loved me and that momma was a crack head and a whore. He said he was going to make sure I was good girl.

I was trapped by daddy. Watching the water rise to the edges of the boat I wanted to jump in. George told me to bend over the edge of the boat and I did. He positioned himself behind me and I heard something fall it was his knife. While he was on top of me bearing down on my back, the water splashing up against the boat I could see deep into the water. I thought I was staring at the bottom of the ocean. The coral and the fish were calling my name. It was a different world, I wanted to be down there with them. Any other place would have been better than being up here with this man called "Daddy" digging into me. The edge of the boat was the only thing keeping me from falling in the water while he kept pushing down on me. I managed to reach down to the bottom of my feet and grabbed daddy's knife. I stared down in my small hand, at the shiny point. I knew it was sharp, I watched daddy cut a fish with it. He would make one swipe motion and its guts would fall out on the floor. I cried for daddy to get off me, but he kept saying "Be my good girl will ya." When he said that my tears dried up. I didn't want to be a good girl anymore. I took the knife and I jabbed it into his leg like I seen him do with the fish. He fell off me in shock. His hands went to his leg and he screamed "What's wrong with you girl! Give me my knife!" reaching out for it. I stood tall over him while he sat at the bottom of the boat holding onto his leg. If he didn't die, I would never be free. I swung my arm down and stabbed him in his stomach. He grabbed his stomach and tried to grab me too but he couldn't get up. I backed up and went in for another stab. I Kept stabbing until daddy wasn't talking or breathing anymore. I swung my arm forty-one times. Daddy just laid there and we floated for a long time. I watched the water rise up and down. I kept looking over the boat hoping somebody was going jump out and save me, nobody came. A day passed and the birds started to come peck on daddy's wounds, they started with his arms and then his head. I couldn't take the smell after two days and I pushed daddy's body off the boat and watched him sink down into the water. I sat in the boat and when the rainstorm came it started to fill up the bottom of the boat. I dumped out the bait and scooped the water out the bottom of it over and over until the blood was gone. I still had daddy's knife. The coast guard didn't find me until three days later. Everybody wanted to know what happen to Daddy, and where were my clothes. Momma tried to get it out of me every day, Taylor never asked. Taylor would just stare at me like she hated me, like I was trash like she knew I killed him. It should have been her he was raping not me. Mama always had her head in the clouds with the stuff he bought her, she never paid attention. George was always perfect in her eyes. When I told her what daddy was doing, she didn't believe me and said baby he was just playing rough, your daddy loves you. I hated mama after that. She chose daddy and drugs over me.

Once I reached home Taylor kept calling. She had moved out of her house and I didn't know where she lived. Last time I was there I almost beat her ass for short changing me with the money daddy left us. Even though he left it in her name and he left it for all of us and I needed more to survive. My job fired me a long time ago for threatening to kill my manager. I didn't have any income coming in and Tori was holding back. I was going to teach her a lesson. Maybe I should get her to go out with me tonight, try to bond with her and take her check book. I want to break her down like she tried to break me. Taylor should have been a better sister and stood up for me when I told her about daddy. I called Taylor back and asked her to meet me at my favorite bar and grill and I will bring some clothes and stuff so we can hang out. She hesitantly agreed to meet but she ended the conversation saying she wasn't going to stay long. I grabbed the clothes and my special sauce I used for Tori for the wine. I wanted us to dress alike so she could feel like we were bonding.

After we arrived at the club I saw Will and teased him for a bit. He remembered my face but not my name. He was acting completely different than earlier. I wanted to tease him to the point of explosion and then push Taylor his way. I wanted him to think I was Taylor. After teasing Will I walked off leaving him on the edge. Taylor was still in the bathroom dizzy and high out of her mind. The drinks I gave her had kicked in. I told her who to walk over to and when she did Will did exactly what I thought he would do. I stood and watching behind a crowd dancing as Will fucked Taylor up against the wall. Shame, she should have believed me when I was a little girl, now no one will ever believe her. Taylor was trying to fight back but she was no match for him. Not a bone in my body wanted to go help her. As I was watching I started thinking what if he does this to Tori. She doesn't even know who she was living with. An idea came to mind, I should run to Tori's house while he wasn't there. I could use my extra key to get in.

I ran out the club and I sped to Tori's house. I had to find something on Will to make her kick him out of her house. She could be staying away from home because of him. I still didn't know where she was at and I called her phone almost every hour, she never answered one call. I pulled up to her place the driveway was empty and the lights in the house were off. I opened the door and crept up to Tori's room. It smelled just like her. It was a sweet smell in the air. I laid on her bed for a minute smelling her pillow, it held the coconut scent of her hair. I went down stairs into the backroom that Will was staying in. when I cracked the door an instant smell of weed came crashing up my nose. He had his clothes neatly stacked in a corner on the dresser and his shoes sat on the side of the bed as if he was ready to jump in them when he woke up. The way he had shit set up screamed jail bird. I peaked in one of the dressers draws and there was nothing in there but a huge zip loc bag full of weed. In the corner of the room next to the closet, there was a suitcase and a duffle bag. Inside the suitcase there was more clothes and a bunch of pill bottles.

More pill bottles in the zip pocket with manila folders and papers. I read one of the documents and it was a letter from a doctor about the treatment of HIV, I was in shock. He looked completely healthy when I saw him, he didn't have any signs that he may be sick. I took a picture of the paper so I can send it to Tori if she doesn't end up replying. Damn, I didn't see him wrap anything up at the club. In the duffel bag there was yet another zip loc bag full of different colored pills. It looked like ecstasy. I took a handful out and put them in my purse. He probably wouldn't know the difference because it was so many. I just hope he didn't weigh the damn thing. I put his stuff back the way I found it and closed Tori's door back, I had everything I needed. The secret was out, Will was selling drugs, I didn't see any business papers in that room. The only papers were of his disease and prison release. Now I just had to find out where Tori was so I could tell her that her boy was a fraud. Will couldn't keep dealing drugs a secret or his HIV status with me around. It was nobody's business, but if he was trying to sleep with Tori, my girl, that's my damn business.

Vanessa Robinson

~Tori~

His Will be Done

It was time for me to go back to my house and see how Will was doing. It had been days since I've spoken with him and he could be worried about me. Dru wanted to ride with me but first we had to stop by the Diner to check on my car. As we pulled up to my car, something didn't look quite right about it. It was leaning to one side. We walked around the car and both tires on the driver's side were jaggedly slashed. This is not what the fuck I needed right now. Instant sensations of fire crept up the back of my neck. My car getting towed and fixed was another stressful thing I'd have to deal with. We walked into the Diner to talk to Mr. Smith, to see if he served the person who did this to my car. Mr. Smith was behind the counter putting pie slices the glass encasement. When he saw me he hobbled from behind around the chairs with his eyes lit up.

"Just who I wanted to see; some light skinned girl came here looking for you" he said in a huff trying to catch his breath.

Her Blood

"Who came here for me? And do you know what happen to my car?" I could barely get the words out.

Mr. Smith motioned for me to sit down in the plastic booth since he had lost his breath. We sat for almost a minute in silence while he swallowed air trying to get himself together. Dru sat beside me with her arm around me waiting for Mr. Smith to speak. We had never sat like this before in public but the events over the last few days were becoming bizarre to me.

"It was a woman; she almost looks like kin to you but a little bit older and a real nasty attitude. She showed me a picture of you on her phone. I gave that lady a piece of pie and she barely touched it—"

"Did she say her name?" I cut him off, he was talking too slow and giving irrelevant information. I couldn't bare to hear one of his tangents about every detail, I needed the facts now.

"Nope she didn't give me her name, she claimed you're her friend and she said you were in some kind of trouble. She knew the sights of your car too." he pointed toward the front patio where my car was parked.

"Mr. Smith my tires are flat on one side of the car do you have cameras out there?" His face turned to an expression of shock and his hands went up in the air.

"Now, Tori that wasn't like that a few days ago, I don't know how that happen."

"Are the camera's outside recording?"

"I have the videos in my back office you could take a look at."

All three of us walked to the back office and re-winded the tapes until we saw someone near my car. There it was, Mae on the camera walking into the Diner and then later busting open the door storming out. Mae walked straight to my car and looked around. She bent down for just a second twice near each tire and then pulled off in her own car. Dru and I thanked Mr. Smith who he made it clear he didn't want no trouble at his Diner. He offered me a key to park the car in the gated back area. Dru helped me push the car in the back, Mr. smith agreed to keep it there until I could tow it.

"Yawl can still come eat pie, but don't bring that woman around here again! Something ain't

right with her." I assured him that I would take care
it.

As I drove the hour to my place, her phone
rang and she said she had to take the call. It was
the friend that she had given the information to
and he needed a few more details from us. My
phone rang too but I figured it was Mae ang
ignored it the first three times. When it rang the
fourth time, I picked it up and immediately the girl
on the other end said "Please don't hang up! I need
to know who the hell you are."

I pulled over and talk to the girl on the line
sounded like she was desperate. Her voice was
familiar and I could've sworn she called me the
other day.

"Who is this?"

"My name is Taylor Moore, I called you once
before to stay away from somebody I know."

"Yeah, but how do you know me? How do
you know Mae? Why would you tell me to stay
away from her?" I didn't even know if I could trust
the voice on the other end, she went silent after
my tirade of questions.

"Hello?" I said. It sounded like the line went dead.

"I'm- I'm here Taylor stammered. Can we meet in person? I rather not have this conversation over the phone?"

"Hold on a second."

Dru was off the phone and before she could say anything, I put the line phone on mute and told her who it was and that she wanted to meet in person.

"Tori you don't have anything to lose, let's see what she has to say" Dru said.

"Yeah, meet me in 30 minutes on the boardwalk."

I gave her the location and I drove a little further and parked in front of the water. Dru grabbed my hand and we sat silently she seemed a little off to me. I had so much energy and thoughts bursting inside me I couldn't stop trembling. A green Mercedes pulled up beside us and a girl stepped out with Hollywood looking sunglasses on. She had long blonde hair and her skin was cocoa brown like mine. When she came close to my window, she pulled down her sunglasses peeking in. Dru and I excited the car. Neither of us spoke, just sized each other up. This woman standing in front of me looked like she could be my twin. Everything about us was the same aside from the obvious hair color and she was slightly shorter than I. Possibly younger by the way she was dressed down, her clothes looked thrown together. I spoke first clearing my throat.

"Are you Taylor?"

"Yes Taylor Moore, I called you earlier. I- I don't know where to start but I think you know Mae? I am trying to find her --"

Dru interjected "Isn't a little odd that you too look just alike?" Her eyes bulging and darting back and forth between us.

Taylor and I just stood there sizing each other up and down. I agree we did favor each other a lot.

"Yes, it's weird but I don't know how we could be related I grew up here and you have an east coast accent." Taylor pointed out.

"Wait a minute Taylor, excuse us for a second."

Dru pulled me to the side, speaking in a hushed tone. "Do you trust her? I received a call from my guy, the investigator."

"What did he say?"

"He said he found some information about Mae. I hate to tell you this, but Mae is somehow related to Lena, your mother. My guy mentioned that Mae has been in and out of psychiatric hospitals since she was a kid. He thinks she is Lena's daughter; she was born in Boston, the same city as you Tori."

"Maybe it's just a coincidence and your intel are wrong, come on Dru I'd recognize my own sister. I'm not blind, especially Mae. This sounds crazy."

"Tori how do you explain this girl just showing up out of nowhere? Yes, this is some wild shit, but it makes sense to me. how else did she get your number?" Dru stopped talking and stared at me for a response.

"Dru I just want the truth." I started to feel sick inside. If Mae was related to my mother or is her daughter that would mean I slept with my sister. I was standing there feeling like I was about to lose my mind. The fire rose up my neck and my head started pounding. Taylor stepped in closer to me.

"I heard you mention my sister and mothers name. How do you know her? What is your relationship to Mae?"

"Mae is my best friend" I said back., my mouth was full of cotton.

"That's my sister, she's out of control and I need to find her. I'm her younger sister and if you look exactly like me, I think I just found out my mother's secret is true." She said bursting into tears.

That was the last thing I remember before everything went black. When I came to my senses, I was in the car and the air conditioner blasting in my face. She was shaking me by the arm and calling my name.

"I'm okay, I just need some water."

Taylor was standing outside of the car crying. I eased out and asked her who her mother was. She began to tell me the rumor of how Lena had a baby when she was on drugs and sold it. She always asked her mother for the truth but her mother would never tell her if I even existed. Taylor told me about Mae and their father George went missing on a fishing trip with just them two. She cried the whole time she was talking, her eyes kept glancing at the birth mark on my face. I noticed she had the same marks on her face. I grabbed my wallet out of the car and took out the picture out of Lena that I carried with me since a child. I passed it to Taylor gently laying it in her hand.

"This is my mother when she was a teenager." Taylor said. I began to cry too, I finally met a piece of me, she was my real family. Dru stood back while Taylor and I hugged for what seemed like forever.

Dru grabbed both of our hands, "I'll drive you two to the hospital, go get a blood test to confirm it. If you too are sisters that means Mae is your sister Tori, she needs to be stopped."

I called my doctor and the three of us headed to the office. My Doctor was astounded at the resemblance we had to each other. The Doctor put an emergency rush on our lab results so we can get confirmation but she had no doubt they would come back conclusive that we were sisters. We held each other's hand while our blood was drawn. I almost cried thinking about finding my family after this chaos. On the outside I was trying not to show any excitement but deep down I was praying she was my sibling. After the test everyone hoped into my car and headed to my house. I didn't want Taylor to leave my side. She was sweet and had a little spice to her too. We shared stories on the ride of how our lives were growing up and where we lived. I told her some things I went through as a child. Dru listened quietly as we both ranted on about our childhood. Taylor wanted to know who raised me. I told her about foster mother Judy. After hearing her name, Taylor gasped and grabbed her chest. I looked in the back and her mouth were hanging open. "What's wrong?"

"Your foster mothers ex-husband is James, that's who Lena had an affair with on George. James used to be a known pimp and drug dealer back in the day and pimped out mommy. He is the one who sold you for money to somebody on the street. Lena is with him now somewhere in a crack house here in LA. I used to think that he was your father but mommy would never answer any of my questions.

"Who told you this?"

"Just heard it from other people growing up, little bits here and there. That would be the only explanation, he has some kind of hold on Lena, I think it's the drugs. When she disappears to get high, she goes right to him selling her body and giving him the money. She comes to me every month or so trying asking for large sums of money looking a mess. Tori, she looks nothing like the woman now, in that picture you have. Her hair is matted and one of her eyes is busted now, she's all outright fucked up. I don't know what happen to her. I don't want to see that woman ever again she isn't in her right mind and doesn't want to be helped."

"I want to ask her why she gave me away like that. Why didn't she come back for me?"

"I don't think Lena is capable of answering you Tori. Every time she came to my house, she robbed me of something. Lena stole whatever she could get her hands on, jewelry, money, toiletries and sometimes my peace of mind. I recently moved and didn't give her my address on purpose. I cut off all contact with her, I don't know where they are. I won't help you find her I refuse to; Lena is dangerous for my health."

Taylor took a deep sigh after speaking and stared out the window. Maybe wished that I was coming into different circumstances and that their family was picture perfect, but they just weren't.

Her Blood

I used to dream about the day I met my mother and the rest of my family. I imagined they would embrace me in their arms and we would have a family dinner. Our hands entwined together praying over the food, praising God that the family was together. Now I realize that was just a silly dream. My whole family was screwed up, even me. My own older sister drugged and raped me and set up her little sister to be raped too. Who knows what else she had done to other people? I was scared for my life. I didn't want to see my own home because it would bring back that horrible day with Mae and the ill feeling that she was actually my half-sister.

As Dru pulled into the driveway, I saw my front door was wide open. I jumped out of the car and towards the house. I made it up the first two steps before Dru grabbed me back by my arm.

"Let me go first Tori, we don't know what we might find."

Dru reached around her back and pulled a small gun from behind her. My throat tightened up, she didn't tell me that she was bringing a gun before we left her house. Dru jogged up the stairs and slid into the front door turning the corner like she was a trained cop. It shocked me how she held the gun and her posture was dead on. Dru demeanor had changed into serious, it could be nothing inside the house. Will may have forgotten to lock the door. Taylor and I waited at the bottom of the steps, she looked worried. An African drum was thumping hard in my chest. I wanted to go in my own house so bad. Dru came sprinting out of the house. "Tori Call 911."

I ran up the steps two at a time to the front door, Dru tried to push me back but I bulldozed my way through knocking her into the doorframe. The living room was ransacked. The canvas black art on the wall was torn down the middle, picture frames of me were smashed and shattered over the floor. My couch was ripped to shreds on the sheets. The pillows appeared chopped with some kind of blade. I walked closer to the kitchen and there was a foul smell coming from the back of the house.

When I stepped in the hallway I started to slide and that's when I realized I was slipping on blood. Looking down at the hardwood floor there was a trail of blood leading from the front to the back of the house. Taking a closer look at the wall I could see splatters of it everywhere. I started to feel the dizziness come over me from the blood. I was in a crime scene, my own house. Dru dragged me out of the house my feet trailing blood back to the door.

Dru had me by the shoulders like she was trying to wake me up while Taylor stood by watching with a horrified look on her face. I didn't know what I had just seen, it looked like something out of a movie.

"This is a crime scene Tori, stay right here until the police come!" she yelled.

I was shaking like I was ice cold. Taylor put her arms around me and warmed me up. The sirens were getting closer to the house. As the police cars turned up the hill, reality hit me, I closed my eyes, "Oh god, I hope no one was dead in my house."

I sat with a blanket around me on the wall of rocks with Taylor; Dru's arms were going up and down explaining to the detectives what she saw. A crowd of people had gathered behind the yellow tape watching with their phones in hand like neighborhood news reporters. A camera man standing a short distance from my house pointed his camera at me and I covered my face. The last thing I wanted was to be plastered on the 5 O'clock news. The police were going in and out the house. I like I was an animal in a zoo, being watched as I tried to keep my emotions together. The men dressed in white protective suits, with slippers wrapped around their shoes wheeled out a bed with a black body bag on top. My Heart sank into my stomach. I ran over to them with Taylor fast on my heels. I needed to see who It was.

The detective stopped me from getting too close and looked me straight in the eyes. "Tori, I'm going to unzip this bag, can you tell me who this is?" I shook my head and he unzipped the body bag in slow motion and instantly my stomach quenched and I felt vomit rising to the top of my throat.

"That's my friend Will, um William Richardson" I said to the police.

His face looked like it was beaten with a hammer. Will's jaw was swollen on one side and his forehead was cut so deep you could see his skull. Taylor looked over my shoulder and a terrified look came over her face, "That's the man that raped me!" she shouted.

I was stunned. Will was a respectable guy, we grew up together. Will would never do something like that, he respected woman. Somebody murdered him in my house and now my sister that I just met is accusing him of rape. This whole day was too much to process. The detectives brought Taylor to the side and she told them everything she knew about Will and that night. I waited on the side with Dru for hours to get approval to enter my house. After the crew wrapped up taking pictures inside, they allowed me access to pack some clean clothes. I walked through my house looking at the mess. The blood on the walls and the drag marks on the floor screamed at me. A dark energy hung in the room. The police came to the conclusion that whoever killed him he knew them personally because there was no forced entry. There were two glasses of wine on the counter and one of them had a lipstick color that didn't belong to me. I couldn't even come up with possible prospects of who that might be. I thought the only person he knew here was me. I guess I couldn't put it past him that he probably knew other people. I was suspicious about his activities and who he was speaking to on the phone a few days ago. The police revealed to us that they found different kinds of drugs in the guestroom, a gun and the possible murder weapons. He was stabbed more than twenty times and beat in his head with a sharp blunt object. Hearing that from the detectives I feared for my safety. I could have been home if I was not with Dru, it scared me to death knowing I could have been there. I gave them the last known numbers I had for Laura and Wills family in Boston. I didn't want to call Wills people myself because it had been so long since I last spoke to them. Laura and I didn't have a smooth relationship, and I didn't want to start one with her from this trauma. The detectives asked us to come down to the station the next day to answer some more questions.

Her Blood

~Taylor~
Killer

I had never saw a dead body before until I saw my rapist. I finally knew his name. William Richardson, my own sisters' lifelong friend. I would never have my moment of whooping his ass myself or telling him what he took from me that night. Somebody else wasted him before I could. I wanted to stab at him too but I couldn't with so many the people around. I guess Tori's friend wasn't a praiseworthy guy after all. Tori looked like she was broken, scared and plain old shocked. After I blurted out he was the man that assaulted me, she barely looks me in the eyes. I get the feeling that she doesn't believe me because of the pedestal she had him on, Will was Tori's hero. I pray his murder didn't have anything to do with Mae, but the evidence didn't look favorable. I hated my Mae for the terrible things she did to people but I don't want to see her on death row. Some part of me sympathized for her, she needed help. I didn't tell the officers that she could be involved because I didn't want them to shoot out of here looking for Mae. I wanted to find that bitch first.

Her Blood

Tori was moping around with a ghostly look on her face. I was afraid to go home alone. After Tori grabbed her things Dru invited me to her house for the night. It seemed like she truly cared about Tori more than just friends but that was none of my business. I could tell she was digging her, Dru shielded her from danger like she was her lover and protector. If Mae knew that, she would be enraged since she was obsessed with Tori. While Tori was in the shower drenching herself in sorrows over Will Dru tried to make small talk with me at the kitchen table. Her body language was awkward, she was stiff and said every word slow and careful as I was deaf and forced to read lips.

"How are you feeling?"

"I'm in shock how else would I feel? I don't want to talk about it, I'm not into sharing."

I had a full-blown attitude in my voice when I answered her. I wasn't in the mood and the answer to that question was common sense to me. She seemed to get the message and turned towards the sink. I didn't need to talk about shit with her and was silent after that. Minutes had passed and I just stared at the randomly placed decorations to keep from making eye contact. It was obvious she was some type of Latin nationality. I was surrounded by different types of hombres and maracas on the wall. There was a mountain of rotten yellow plantains in a basket on the counter. Dru had jet black shiny wavy hair and an olive brown skin color. On the fridge was a picture of an older Latin woman smiling with an apron on hugging a teenage boy. The people in the polaroid photo looked like her family, they had the same slanted eyes and smile. There was a quote written underneath the picture that read in Spanish, *"El tiempo dedicado a la familia vale cada",* I tried to translate the words in my head but I couldn't. I never paid attention in Spanish class but I knew it said something about family and time. Dru saw me studying the photo and turned away again like I was prying into her life. I assumed she didn't want any questions either.

It started to feel awkward as hell sitting there without the presence of Tori in the room. I didn't know anything personal about Dru aside that she was my sisters' friend. Tori was my blood and I didn't know her either except what she told me about herself. I believed with my whole heart we were related just by the details she gave me about her past. I can't stop wondering how could Tori not know that Mae was related to her too. We all looked alike juxtaposed together, Tori and I were more twins, except she had birthmarks exactly like mom. Lena had strong genes, that carried over to the three of us. Mae was much older and had Georges big nose, but we still had some of the same features that could indicate we were related. Tori had to take some blame in being naive, not at least questioning the looks. If Mae was her best friend like she says, why didn't she know anything about her past or seen any childhood photos at least. Something should have given her the red flag that crazy ass Mae was not being honest. It popped into my mind maybe Tori was so wrapped up in her own world she couldn't see reality of what was happening right before I her eyes. Tori looked like she had everything she could ever want. She lived in an upscale neighborhood and her house didn't look cheap. Dru was fawning over her every move but Tori had her in the friend zone. I could see she was paid just by the diamond necklace she had around her neck. The material of her clothes were dope designer brands that I circle in magazines and dream to afford one day. I wonder how she could be so stupid and let Mae and Will fuck up her life.

Tori walked into the kitchen dressed in a tank top and tight yoga pants. Her simple outfit hugged each of her round curves and she smelled like coconuts, her wild big afro of curls bouncing on her head with every step she took. Dru stood leaning back on the kitchen counter with her head down but when Tori walked in the room she stood straight up, her eyes gazing up and down her body. Tori sat down at the kitchen table across from me and folded her arms. Her eyes were slightly red, it looked like she had been crying in the shower.

"Taylor, I want you to call Mae now. I want to put an end to this!" The look on her face was serious and from the sound of her voice she was angry and tired.

"Are you sure? she isn't stable, and she hasn't picked up any of my calls," I said.

"I'm serious as a fucking heart attack! If she doesn't answer leave her a message and tell her you're with me. I want her to know that, I know who the fuck she really is! I want you to call Lena too.

"Shit, you're asking for a lot sis, I'm not sur—" Tori cut me off.

"I want to see her for myself, I want to see the woman who gave me away for crack and a pimp. I had enough of my blood lying and hiding things from me."

Her Blood

Tori's face turned deep red under her tender brown skin, Tori was serious. I knew if I didn't make the phone call in front of her, she might not trust me too. I picked up my phone and dialed Mae's number.

"And tell that bitch to meet us tonight on the boardwalk across from Smith Diner where she slit my fucking tires!" Tori added.

I put the phone on speaker, Mae answered on the first ring.

"Hey Sis!! I see you had a risqué night at the club the other day" Mae laughed.

I was appalled this bitch thought being raped in a club was funny. A rageful wave of heat creeping up the back of my neck. Mae was such an awful person when she wasn't on her medication. I didn't know who she had become, she acted like a monster.

"Fuck you Mae, you had Will rape me! How do you live with yourself, you're sick and you need help!" Spit flew out of my mouth when I said that. She was laughing on the other end of the phone like she was at a comedy show.

"Well now you know how it was when daddy used to be on top of me bitch, welcome to the club." She was clapping her hands in the background.

"Listen you sick twisted bitch, I should have never trusted you!!! Guess who I'm with? Your best friend Tori, oh no wait your sister Tori, remember her?"

Mae went silent for a second and I could hear her breathing hard into the phone.

"You're a liar, I'm not falling for your bullshit, how do you know Tori?" Mae said.

"Never mind that, meet me at the boardwalk tonight across from Smith Diner. Make sure you bring our rotten mother with you, crazy bitch. You know where she lives."

Tori held up ten fingers in front of me to tell her the time. "Be there at ten o'clock!" I hung up the phone and we both just cried while Dru watched. I looked at both of them and said "We need to pray for our blood. Pray for our twisted soul sister."

Her Blood

Vanessa Robinson

~Lena~

Stains on the Mattress

James was up to his bullshit again, he never listened to me. I was laid out on the mattress looking out the window smoking a cigarette. I should have known James was up to no good when I saw the pistol print in his back before he left the house. James came running down the street through the yard dragging his fucked-up leg. He bust in the door with a whole lot of twenty-dollar bills in his hand. James claimed that some lady down at the corner store left her purse on the counter and he took the money out and the credit cards. According to him it only took a minute, but I know better. I thank he was snatching purses again. We were falling on hard times and I couldn't work because the last trick threw my back out. This fool still wanted me to work but I couldn't even bend down. For the last two days I been laid in this bed chasing the dragon to ease the pain. I was getting too old to be naked spilled over the yard fucking for money. Laying here counting the dirty stains on the bed was better than grass. James sat down and

picked up the pipe and started to blow, that's just
what I needed.

"Why you out in them streets robbing folks?
You gon' get locked up!"

"Shut up! I need money for your medicine
since your big broke up ass can't work!"

"I'll be better soon; I just need a break. When
are you going to get us out of here. You been
saying the same old shit for years James. I'm tired."

"You ain't find Taylor yet gal? If she was still
holding you up, I wouldn't have to be out there in
the streets robbing folks."

James blew the smoke out his mouth and
passed it to me to pull. Here we go again with his
lies. I knew she would cut me off one day but not
like this. She just disappeared, no message or
nothing. The little bitch think she is perfect and
better than her own mother. Telling me to check
back into rehab, I didn't see a reason to. I was living
my life just the way I wanted with my man. She
wouldn't let me move in again because she says I
steal her things. I think she just misplaced shit in
her own house or maybe some man she was
dealing with stole her jewelry. Maybe it's one less

burden that she's gone, she won't help me do anything anyway. Taylor looks down on me and shake her head and say "What would George think of you now?"

"George is gone girl, let your father rest in peace. He can't look for me if he dead. I wouldn't want him to see me like this anyway." Taylor knew all the right things to say to hurt me. It brought back bad memories of the last time George saw me high living this life. It's ironic that Taylor is the one to throw it up in face if he saw me like this because that's exactly how she was conceived.

Last time George did, when I sat in that car and thought he was a trick, he almost killed me. When that Cadillac pulled up, I had no idea I was George. I heard the doors lock and when I looked up it was George. I was so shocked my wig fell off. I tried to get out but he grabbed the back of my head and slammed it into the dashboard. He punched me in my face so many times I couldn't see. George ran around to my side car and yanked me out to the ground by the little bit of real hair I had left on my head. He dragged me to the trunk skinning up my whole back. I was kicking my legs and hollering for James to help me. I didn't know what George was fixing to do to me. I had betrayed him and turned him into a killer. James came running to car with his gun in his hand. That was the first time I seen that look in George eyes like he wanted to kill James. George told him to back the fuck up or he would stomp me to death. George held up his foot over me and all I could see was the grooves on the bottom of his big black boots. I had just had the baby that James took away, I couldn't even fathom the pain if he started stomping on my stomach. I screamed out for James to just leave and let me handle this. George pulled me up by hair and threw me half-way in the trunk and started having sex with me right there. James stood there and watched, his lips shaking like he was the one being beaten. James kept throwing his body forward like he wanted to jump on George but he didn't move a foot off the ground.

James was shaking his head back and forth mumbling "You bastard, she doesn't love you."

George was pumping me saying "This is my wife muthafuckah."

I didn't see James for years after that incident, I went home with George. Three months later we moved to California when I found out I was pregnant with Taylor. I got pregnant on that trunk because he saw me like this. I had to be the prefect wife with George but I was so freeling with James.

Taylor didn't know any better she'd hate her daddy if I told her...... I hit the pipe again and it started to crackle.

James laid his head back next to me right on top the yellow big stain. He kept clearing his throat and
snorting like he couldn't breathe. His nose crinkled up and twisted, he blew straight out his nose with no tissue and the green landed on the bed, just another stain. James didn't have no home training, he was just plain old nasty. Looking at him made me think about the baby girl he took away. With the dragon in my blood it gave me the courage to ask him what he did with my baby.

"James remember that night when you took the baby away from me? What did you do with her?" I said it so matter-of-factly, I didn't want him to think I was trying to argue.

"What damn baby? I don't remember no damn baby!" he yelled out.

"James please, I know it's been thirty-five years but don't play dumb on me today, acting like you don't remember isn't going to change a thing. Just tell me, I have the right to know."

"Shit if you want to know so bad you should have kept her!" He spat back. "You gave up your rights so I gave her to Judy. She couldn't have any kids and she kept begging me for a baby while we was married, so I brought her evil ass one."

I was numb, Judy was James now ex-wife but back then, when we started fooling, they were still married. James kept on talking under his breath to himself, like he was confessing. I guess that little push made him want to get stuff off his chest. He pounded his fist into his legs while he was talking in between snorts.

"This is the only and the last time I'm going tell you Lena. I told Judy, if she takes the baby and adopt her, we would get back together. I told her to tell the people that she found the baby on the bench so they won't come after me for child support. When I was there, I told her it was a charge to keep the child, she gave me three months of rent from her out her closet. Once she agreed to keep the baby, I told her I was going to the store for a pack of cigarettes. I never went back home. Judy was mad and threatened me that she would tell the authorities I was the daddy but she never did. Judy knew she would have gone to jail for taking a baby without papers. I heard she recruited a lady to make up a birth certificate so she can get a check every month. Judy knew she couldn't have kids that's why she became a drunk. Every time I turn around when I called the house, she was drunk as a skunk. Every weekend she was over there drinking forty ounces and cheap cognac mixed together, yelling at that girl for nothing. I sent Dodie over there to tell her to cut that shit out! That little girl ain't did nothing to her."

After his rant he sat there with his shoulders hunched over like he was staring into dead space. I knew he was a hustler, but he hustled his then wife to take care of the baby. James had lied to me and told me he gave her to a stranger. I would have never imagined it to be his ex-wife. She must have been so happy she kept my baby away from me. If I'd of known she was beating her cause I took her man, I would've killed her. I'm glad I had him, I didn't want the baby no way. In the mornings when I get a sober mind, I think about her sometimes. The baby had a sweet face, she looked just like me, birthmarks and all. That child, they are imprinted in me, I don't even know her name. I didn't want any more kids after her because it broke my heart. I was broken, I messed up my marriage and my family. I had Taylor for George, after what he did behind that trunk, I knew I was pregnant when it was happening, George never missed. I thought that would fix me but it didn't, I still was in love with James.

Her Blood

I was laying there in them stains, living inside my head. My phone rang and it was Mae calling. I didn't like to deal with her but I had to, she had a demon inside of her. Whenever Taylor didn't give me no money, she would give me some of hers but not without losing my dignity first. She called me every kind of drug addict and no good momma name in the world. She blamed me for the things she says George did, but I don't believe her. I tried so hard to help her but it wasn't enough, she was a wayward child. Nothing I did would make her behave like a little girl supposed to. Mae would run away from school and lie just about everything under the sun. I caught her trying to set the house on fire with me in it one time. I was sleeping one summer afternoon; Mae had set some books on fire in the basement and ran out the house. I woke up to clouds of smoke in the living room and I ran and put the fire out. I found Mae in the front yard staring at the house like she was waiting for it to burn down. I asked Mae what happen she shrugged her shoulders with the matches tucked in the palm of her hand. She was such a troubled child back then and now she is a troubled grown woman; I don't feel guilty I couldn't get her the right help, the doctors prescribed medicine but none of it would take. Mae tries to beat me down her words every time she comes around.

I let her call go to the voicemail, James turned around and said "Hey, call that crazy girl back, I need some money."

I rolled my eyes and gave him the middle finger behind his back. I was careful to do it after he turned around because the last time, I flipped him off he broke my middle finger. Mae called back before James could call her. I picked up on the first ring "I hope you calling because you have something for me beside drama, I need some money!"

"Old bitch your life is a ghetto soap opera. Look, I'm going to come pick you up and were going to meet up with Taylor. I think she might have something for you. I can't make no promises though she hung up the phone real fast" Mae said.

"My hair ain't done can you bring me one of your wigs and a drink when you pick me up?"

"Momma, Taylor done see your baldheaded ass plenty of times, I'm not bringing you shit. You always want something from somebody! If you stop running these streets and letting these men make you lay on ringworm infested grass to fuck you would have hair! I will be there to pick you up by eight o' clock. Make sure you stand on the corner cause I'm not driving up to that house with them desperate people hanging in the yard begging."

"Little Bitch!" but she already hung up.

I couldn't stand her, she thought she was better than me. I lifted up off the bed and started to get dressed. I guzzled down the pint James bought from the store. I couldn't deal with both of my daughters in the same place being sober. The girls constantly fought looked to me like it was my fault. I didn't want to deal with none of their mess but if Taylor had some money for me, I was going to take it. James ran off the bed to answer the knock on the door, he yelled my name long and hard from the bottom of the stairs. I knew that meant there was a trick down stairs for me. I put on a sundress and no underclothes and limped down the stairs. It was Black, one of my regulars, his old ass didn't have no stamina. As soon as he laid on top of me, he was done in three minutes, sweating and breathing hard. Mae would be here in an hour, so I had time to freshen up. I walked to the back yard and laid down on the mattress.

~Tori~

Guns & letters

I was ready to get this over with. I wasn't going to allow Mae to fuck over my life and run me out of this new place I call home. The steaming water ran down my back making my skin burn. In the shower, I reflected back on our friendship and I realized that she was never my friend. Everything that we did and whenever we spent time together, she was always in control of us. Mae ran the friendship and planned every second of our time together, I could never say no or change things around. I gave her the power over me without even realizing it. I gave her a key to my house for God sake, I trusted her with everything. I legit thought she was my friend and became like family after three years of knowing her. I was scrubbing so hard in the shower, the water was piping hot, it burned my skin. I wanted to get her out of my system, out of my spirit.

I could hear talking outside of the bathroom. Dru was probably trying to talk to Taylor to get more information about my family. Dru wasn't too savvy on small talk, she had some type of social issue that made things awkward. Majority of people she tried to converse with, didn't have much of a response back. Either they were trying to figure out if she was male or female or scared to respond because her conversation always came off as an interrogation. I knew her heart and her mind somewhat and she was just a curious person who wanted to get to know people deeper than a surface level. I tuned them out for a minute and started to think hard, taking in deeps breaths of steam and the natural coconut lavender body wash. I wanted closure; I wanted more answers from my blood relatives. I needed to see Mae face to face and ask her if she knew she was my sister. On many different occasions I shared with her how I wanted to find my family and discussed my upbringing with her. I could have sworn one time I showed her Lena's picture but I can't put my finger on when I did. The memory is foggy, I had no recollection of showing Mae. Perhaps I just want to remember that I did show her, so I can put this shit to rest, so I could know for sure. I wanted confirmation that she is a sicko and then I can move on with my life.

After my shower I sat at the kitchen table across from Taylor, she looked like me, her facial expression was somber. I stared at her facial features while she was looking down scrolling through her phone, it was like looking in the mirror. I wanted to ask her more about Will and if she was okay but I couldn't bring myself to ask. I didn't want to remind her of the alleged rape incident. I just wanted to get the Mae situation over with before I tried to connect with her. I wanted to trust her but I didn't know her. I have no idea how to be a sister. I never had a family connection, I always longed for one and I didn't want to mess it up. Some day we could possibly have a healthy relationship with each other and forget about all of this madness. I needed to make sure she was on my side. I kept staring at her until she looked up, when our eyes met, I saw that hers were teary. I needed Taylor to call Mae and set up a meeting. I wanted Mae to know that Taylor was with me so I can get under her skin. I wanted to make her tick so I could see how she would move. I had her set up a meeting at the Diner down the street. The Diner was a safe place, I knew where all the doors and cameras were if anything shady was going to go down. I planned to get there early to make sure that I put Mr. Smith on guard and have him record everything on the boardwalk across from his diner.

I went in the room where I had dumped my stuff from my place. I had only brought a few outfits and shoes with me. I took my leather jacket and a shirt out of the bag and mail started sliding out of my knapsack with it. I remembered I had grabbed the mail before leaving my house, the crime scene, since I had not been home in a few days. A piece of mail stuck out to me that was laying on top of the covers as I pulled up my pants. It was a white envelope and at the tip of it there was a deep brownish red stain, looking closer it was a finger print of blood. I didn't remember the mailbox being open when I grabbed the mail but I probably wasn't paying attention with everything that was going on. There was no way this could have gotten blood on it unless the person that put it in the mailbox had blood on their fingers. My mailbox was a closed box but it was not locked so anyone could open it and put mail inside. My name was scribbled on the front of it, I sat on the bed, in my bra and opened up the envelope. It was a letter addressed to me but there was no return address on it. The words looked like it was written in a hurry because of the way they floated off the page.

Vanessa Robinson

Tori,

I tried to get to you sooner but I didn't have any of your contact information. I went through Dodie for your address, she didn't want to give it to me but that old heifer was concerned about her fuck boy grandson. For a month she hadn't heard from him. Your place was the only place that I could think of that he would run to. I know you think or thought you knew that sorry excuse for a man but you don't know him anymore. He walked out of jail and left me to clean up his shit, but I have fixed that now. He took the money and even stole Dodies social security retirement money. If you haven't figured it out already this is Laura. Remember me bitch? Anyway, Will was in jail for check fraud. His ass was cashing checks with his crooked crack head friends from Roxbury. The only reason he ended up with you is because nobody wants his ass in Boston and he is wanted for questioning for having sex with a sixteen-year-old Puerto Rican girl. He was scared me and her family were going to kill his ass! Oh, they want fucking blood. He infected me with AIDS. YES, I have FULL Blown AIDS now and my son too. He thought I had an abortion but I didn't. I just had my baby two weeks ago and he tested positive. One day someone will tell him how I beat his father's face in for ruining his life before he even had a chance. That sick fuck was running these

*streets taking hard working people's money,
rapping their daughters and giving then STDS. I feel
so bad for you if you contracted it too! I know he
still wanted you. That's why I never liked you when I
loved him because I knew at any time you could
take him. Will was never mine and that bitch will
never breath again. I stabbed him as many times as
I could so he could feel how many holes he put in
my heart. I fucking hate him. He took my chance
from me to be a mother to my son. I only have a
few months to live, no way I was going to let him
walk around this earth after my death. I hope you
get check homegirl. Sorry about your house.*

    -- L

Shit. I sat there in absolute shock; I didn't
even realize it but my leg was trembling. My skin
was burning underneath. "Boom, Boom" there was
a banging at the bedroom door and it made me
jump back.

"You decent?" Dru was banging on the door.

"Yeah come in." I grabbed the shirt off the
bed, I noticed the letter laying open on the bed, I
snatched it up and folded it up cuffing it in my
hand. I didn't want Dru to read the letter or see it. I
wasn't ready for another episode of chaos I

couldn't control. I never kept anything from her before but I needed a moment to process it. Dru stood in the doorway for a second staring at me and I realized I needed to put my shirt on. She had never seen me without a top on and she stood there looking at my breast mesmerized.

She stuttered a little bit when she spoke "It's getting close to that time to go. Are you okay? Did you get any phone calls?"

"No, nothing, I'm fine" I said backing up, accidently tripping on my shoes. I sat at the edge of the bed and put my head down. I reached into my purse and passed the letter to Dru. She stood there and read the whole thing in under a minute. She handed it back to me and sat down beside me. Her voice was just under a whisper "Does your sister Taylor know that she has been exposed to HIV?"

I shrugged my shoulders slightly taking a deep breath. "Tori you need to tell her. I know you have a lot going on right now but she needs to know. We need to go to the police with this."

I just sat there in silence. I couldn't even fucking talk because everything I thought I knew about the guy I grew up with was a lie. I knew something was going on when he came down here but I didn't think it would be all of this. Statutory rape, purposely infecting young girls with HIV, fraud, weapons, the drugs they found in my house, stealing. Laura killing him and confessing to me in a letter was another bizarre thing, there had to be more to this story. My mind started racing. Dru nudged me in my side trying to snap me out of my thoughts.

"We have to leave now. If you want to cancel the meeting its okay. You need to let me know immediately so Taylor can call and tell them not to come."

I stood up and leaned against the door crossing my arms, "Dru, I do want to go through with this, I'm just a little fuzzy right now. Everything that's been going on is coming to a head and it's a lot to deal with."

"Are you scared to meet your mother?"

"I'm fucking terrified. I know she isn't anything I imagined her to be my entire life. I'm trying to talk myself into being disappointed before I even get there."

"It's okay Mami, I'm your family too and I would never let you down."

I wanted to burst out in a cry but I held it in. I was so tired of being emotional about everything.

Dru jumped up, off the edge of the bed and grabbed me. She put her arms around my waist and next thing I know she was kissing me. Her warm fingertips caressed the small of my back. Dru's lips were pillows of velvet on top of mine, she kissed me gently for a few seconds and then let me completely go. I knew she cared for me but I didn't know it was more than just that. I straightened my top and wiped off my lips.

Dru instantly apologized when she saw how uncomfortable I was. "Sorry I--, I just thought that--" I waved my hand over to stop her from talking, this just wasn't the right time. I didn't want to respond regarding the kiss because I couldn't even process it. I liked Dru a lot but the last thing I wanted to do was ruin our friendship over a kiss. I already lost one person dear to me and was heading to lose another.

"Let's go, Taylor is probably wondering what we are doing." I opened the door and there Taylor was standing behind it. I gasped not knowing if she heard what we were talking about. I didn't know how long she'd been standing there listening and she looked just as startled as me with her eyes bulging.

"Are you ready to go?" she shook her head yes. I grabbed Dru's car keys and Taylor followed behind me and Dru setting the alarm behind us. While we were walking to the car, I started thinking it might be better if Taylor is the one who waits for them and then Dru and I walk up. I didn't want them to think that we were there to gang up on them. As Dru drove to the diner the car was silent, not even the radio was playing. She had a worried look on her face, I don't think her forehead could've wrinkled up any harder. Even though she was driving a short distance, she seemed unfocused on the road almost swerving into the curb. I knew she was thinking about us and worried I may not feel the same about her. I rested my hand lightly on her thigh and gave it a meaningful squeeze to assure everything was cool. She looked over at me and gave half a smile. I was grateful that she was here with me because none of this shit was her problem and she didn't have to be here having my back. We parked a few restaurants down from the Diner. I went in to talk to Mr. Smith and let him know to turn on the cameras to record, he was confused as to why but I told him to trust me and I would tell him later, just keep making those pies. Before I walked out the door, he called my name and waved me back but Taylor swung the door open and said they just pulled up to the board walk and she was going over. I wanted her to wait to tell her something but I couldn't catch her in time. I walked over to the car where Dru stood smoking a cigarette. I had no idea she smoked cigarettes.

"When did that start?" I asked her, peering down at the cancer killer. I leaned back against the car with her, picked it out of her hand and took a pull of it. She laughed nervously and asked me the same question back. After my second pull I threw it on the ground and stepped on it. I could see Mae get out of the car and walk around to greet Taylor. The car door opened on the front passenger side and the woman getting out looked shorter and heavy set. The woman used the door for assistance to get out of the car. As I begin walking up to their car, I started to hear yelling, it was Mae's voice, she pushed Taylor in her chest with both hands. I ran up to them both and stood in front of Taylor. My heart danced in my chest and everything around me froze. The woman beside Mae was my mother indeed. She didn't have much hair on her head, it was salt and pepper mixed together and her edge were a memory. Her eye that Taylor had mentioned was nearly closed and dragged down on her face as if she had a stroke. She was nothing like the woman in the picture I kept close to my heart my whole life. Her youth looked snatched from her by demons from hell. The image of my mother was torn from of me by the sight of her standing before me. Mae standing next to her looked like she hadn't combed her hair in days. We made eye contact, her face went from angry to soft, as if seeing me had calmed her from the deadly glare at Taylor.

I looked at Lena and I asked her directly "Did you have a baby girl on September 4th 1984?". She stared at me and walked a little closer and said "Yes I did."

"Do you know that I am your daughter?" I asked, my eyes locked on hers. She looked me up and down and responded, "By the looks of it, ye-yes, I think you are." She stuttered while she talked, she seemed a little nervous. I didn't feel anything like I thought I would while speaking to her. I thought I would want to hug her or feel something more than the anger that pulsated through me. It was confirmation that Mae was my sister and I was completely disgusted by the both of them. They were just standing there staring at me like I was a fool. I reached behind me and I took the gun I had tucked from waistband and pointed it at my mother. This bitch gave birth to me and then threw me away like trash. I pointed it directly into Lena's face. Her eyes watered while she stared into the barrel of the gun.

"Why did you give me away like a piece of trash?", my hands were shaking, my finger was on the trigger. Rain began to fall from the sky, droplets of water mixed with my tears. Lena began to mumble something, shaking her head back and forth. Dru was stood close behind me "Tori please put the gun down, you can sit down and talk to your mother, all of them. Please don't do this Tori, this isn't you."

This was me. I waited for so long to meet my family and here they were. These people were robbing me of my happiness stalking me, stealing my peace from me. I knew my mother would never love me. Lena never wanted me; she was too lost. I wanted to them hurt the way I did when I was a child. Mae eased over to Lena with her hands out in front her body, she was slowly pushing her mother out of the view of my gun. She tried to speak like we were still friends but that shit was not going to work on me. I didn't want to hear anything this bitch had to say. She drugged me and took advantage of me, what kind of woman was she? I closed my eyes, my whole body was shaking, at this point I didn't know who I had the gun pointed at. I pulled the trigger twice and instantly dropped the gun after firing it. Taylor let out a siren sounding scream. Dru grabbed my shoulder and yanked me back. When I finally opened my eyes, Lena was down on the ground with her hand over her chest, her eyes wide and Mae kneeling over her. "I think she's having a heart attack." I didn't see any blood seeping from underneath her hand. I realized I actually didn't shoot anyone. The gun scared her so bad she had fallen to the ground in cardiac arrest. Dru had to nearly drag Taylor away because she was in hysterics. The ambulance came and carried Lena away while Mae stood there watching me with a smirk on her face as Dru pulled off. Dru brought me back to her place and gave me a valium. I fought my sleep through my tears, I didn't know who I had become.

When I opened my eyes, the sunlight was peering through the windows. I turned over and Taylor was lying next to me curled in a ball. My whole body was heavy and drained from the night before. In the living room Dru sat on the sofa with a steaming cup of coffee, watching the news on silent.

"Dru I'm sorry about last night I completely lost it." She looked up at me and shook her head up and down in agreement. She stayed silent and put her eyes back on the TV. I didn't know what else to say, her head shake was enough, I didn't want to push for more. Looking through my phone, a message from Mae read "Killer, Mommy dearest is dead, you the real MVP." I tapped Dru on the leg and showed her my phone and she just shook her head back and forth.

"I think I should confess to the police, I killed her. Lena wouldn't have had that heart attack if weren't for me pointing that gun in face and shooting it."

"It's not your fault Tori, she could've already had issues with her heart and blaming yourself isn't going to make it better." Dru stood up and turned the television off.

"Can I talk to you in the kitchen about something." I followed her and sat at the kitchen table while she stood at the counter.

"We need to go to the police about the letter, before we go, I think you need to let Taylor know what she is up against."

"I'm scared to tell her; she has been through a lot this last week and the letter just might break her."

"Tori we all have been through it this week; wouldn't you want to know if it were you?"

"Yeah, I would, I mean he was my friend, like family. I don't want her to think I was involved or be upset with me. I want to have a relationship with her—" as I said that Taylor came in the kitchen, her eyes were puffy and red.

"Just tell me what is, I heard you talking about me from the room. After last night I think I can handle anything." She looked back and forth between both of us. Dru stood there staring at me.

"Alright." I retrieved the letter from the room, before I handed it to Taylor I needed to know if this was going to forward. "Promise me that we will all go to the police today." She nodded her head.

Taylor dropped the letter after a minute and slid down the kitchen wall crying knocking pictures off the wall. I ran over to her and put my arms around her and just rocked as she cried. I wasn't prepared for this; I began to cry with her. I could feel the pain seeping out of her into me. Taylor didn't ask for this and her own sister set her up. None of us asked for this. Mae needed to be in jail for doing all of this especially for Taylor since she was dealt the worst of it.

Taylor stopped sobbing and stood up in a daze. "Let's go, I want to go to the police station now." Dru and I exchanged looks and I followed behind Taylor into the guest bedroom to get dressed. We headed out the door and I hoped in the driver seat. The car was deadly silent aside from Taylors sniffling. It sounded like she could hardly breath back there. I opened the sunroof letting the oceans breeze through the window I said prayers for her in my head over and over. Life was so short and hers may have just become shorter. My mind started to wonder, I couldn't help but think what if I did choose to fuck Will and he knowingly gave me HIV. I would want to kill him myself, a part of me wasn't even mad at Laura for stabbing him to death

Her Blood

Vanessa Robinson

~Mae~

Blood in my Pie

Mommy dearest was gone. After Tori's little show and Taylors antics at the beach, I went to the bar and had a neat drink. I rode with mommy in the ambulance while she laid there not moving. The paramedics tried to revive her but it was a waste of energy. After I told her she was going to meet the daughter she threw away she lost it. Lena couldn't stop hitting her pipe on the way to the boardwalk she was so nervous, I guess it grasped the best of her. I hid my smile the whole pitiful bumpy way to the hospital. I only took the ride to make sure that she was dead. I loved her once upon a time, but ever since I knew that she didn't care what daddy did to me, I wanted her to suffer. Lena was going to hell for turning a blind eye to my abuse. Once she was buried, I'm going to go stomp on her grave. Lena didn't have long to live anyway with all the different drugs and drinking she did. I called James and told him that his precious little daughter gave Lena a heart attack. I didn't hold the phone long enough to hear his reaction. I could tell he was high as a kite because he hardly knew who I was. James could follow up with Taylor because I blocked his number.

Seeing Tori and Taylor together last night pissed me off. I hope they weren't thinking they were going to have the perfect sisterly relationship and leave me out. The hairs on the back of my neck curled up when Tori stood in front of me. I could smell her coconut shampoo, the coca butter smell of her skin mixing with the beach salt water on the tip of my nose. I loved Tori, if nobody knew she was my sister we could be together. It's not like we were real sisters. We didn't have the same father and Tori was never a part of the family. Those two alone should cancel out the maternal blood relation. I saw her little girlfriend with her, I think it was her girlfriend. The way she came up close trying to convince Tori not to shoot Lena, let me know they knew each other well. Taylor tried to fight me like she was tough all of a sudden. I told her I would slit her throat if she ever tried to come at me again. Little sis was a weak ass little girl. When I pushed Taylor on the beach, I stuck a little tracker on her jacket. It was just a small dot that tracks the area location she's in. I was on my way to her location now to see where she was staying. The tracker led me right back to the board walk from last night. I was praying that it didn't fall off her jacket. The tracker was beeping and that meant she was on the move. It was coming right towards me; the noise was getting louder and faster. Taylor must be in a car heading somewhere.

The car coming the opposite way slowed down at the stop sign in front of me. Looking deep into the car I saw Tori and her friend in the front and Taylor sitting in the back with her head down. It took everything in me not to ram my car into theirs so they could taste the airbag dust. Tori's looked me right in the eyes and sped off from the corner jumping the curb. I didn't want them to get out of my sight but I knew they would see me following them in broad daylight. The side street they were coming from was a small community of spread out beach houses. I could park somewhere and start knocking on doors to see which house they came from. I wanted Taylor and Tori's friend out of the picture. I didn't know who she was but I had unfinished business with Tori. We never had the opportunity to talk about our friendship. I wasn't going to let her put me out of her life this easy. I had to deal my cards right or everything I planned will crumble.

I turned the car around and headed to the diner to make sure that old man deleted the tape. I knew he had cheap cameras back there watching the diner. I purposely showed myself on camera slitting Tori's tires so she could get my message that I just wasn't going to give up. If the police saw the tape from last night, they'd be looking for me. I already had a warrant for my arrest in Texas. Damon, my ex-boyfriend took out a restraining order on me and I violated it. I went up to his job and poured bleach all over his BMW seats and cut some cords underneath the hood. I could've have sworn he was cheating on me and followed him everywhere he went to catch him in the act. When I couldn't catch him, I messed up his car to see if a woman would come and pick him up. Damon called the police and tried to have me arrested but they had no proof I vandalized the car. That following day I was served with a restraining order. I went to his house to talk to him and he pushed out the door and locked it. I set his house on fire. I ran from Texas and went back to California. I tried to tell the police it was a misunderstanding over the phone but they claimed I violated a restraining order and would arrest me on site.

A horn blared at me as I drove into the entrance of the Diner almost side swiping my passenger side. Patrons sitting in the patio dining area gawked from under their color umbrellas at the almost collision.

Vanessa Robinson

I walked into the Diner and the old man was sitting at the first booth through the door eating that nasty ass pie he gave me the other day. I can't believe he is allowed to serve people garbage for money. When he looked up from his pie, he recognized me and tried to get up fast from the table towards the back office. I let him hobble away, he looked like he was running to the bathroom trying to hold his shit in. I smiled at people following behind him into the hall, I didn't want anyone to be alarmed. In the hallway he backed up against the door, holding onto the knob.

"Open the fucking door, old man"

"No Miss lady, I can't do that because you're not an employee here and I have important documents back there. I'm going to have to call the police." He tried to step around me, but I stood in front of him and pushed the five-hundred-thousand-watt stun gun into his side.

"You know if I stun you with this, your ancient heart isn't going to make it. "OPEN THE FUCKING DOOR!" I pushed a little harder into his ribs and he opened the door backing into the room. I motioned for him to sit in the chair in front the cameras.

"I don't have money in here, it's just papers, this Diner doesn't make a lot of money Miss —"

Her Blood

I went close to his ear because I wanted him to hear me clearly. "Shut the fuck up and do what I tell you to do. Pull the tape from yesterday and delete all of it."

"I don't know how to do that. My—My grandson do everything for me on the computer."

I hit him over his head with my fist and his eyes rolled back into his head a little bit. Out of the three monitors, two of them were CCTV for the diner and the property outside and the other one was playing a Spike Lee movie. Mr. Smith sat down at the computer circling his finger over the keyboard like a pendulum. I thought he was lying when he said he didn't know how to work the thing.

"Move, I'll do it myself since you want to play stupid." I pushed him over he fell out of the chair onto the floor with his hands up in the air.

"Such a pretty lady like you, have a cold heart, what is you doing all this for, huh?"

"I do what needs to be done." Looking down at his desk there were papers stacked up on top of each other. On the top there was a letter from some cancer institute and on another was a screenshot of me from the CCTV camera and my name scribbled on it.

"So, you plan on turning me in old man?"

"Yeah you're a criminal and you ain't supposed to be here. I'm going to call the police and you're going to go to jail. I know what you been doing you won't get away with this. Tori don't want nothing to do with you."

He just had to piss me off. I moved close to his face so he could hear. "Watch your fucking mouth. You don't have long with that type of cancer you have right? I'm going to help you out and send you to hell now."

Mr. smith put his hands up to block me when I stood up over him. I stomped on his chest and stomach until he stopped screaming. I deleted the video tape and turned the cameras off completely. I grabbed the papers off the desk and wiped the red off my shoes on the mat by the door and slipped out the restaurant. I couldn't risk him calling the police on me. I sure as hell wasn't going to jail because he couldn't mind his fucking business.

Her Blood

~Tori~

Gun powder

A migraine crept up the back of my neck like a vice grip beginning to wrap around my head. Dark energy hovered heavy over me after telling the detectives everything I knew about Will, Laura and Mae. They asked me questions about Mae. I revealed to them she was involved in the assault on her sister, everything spilled out about what went down over the last week. I even told them Mae was now stalking me. The officer looked shocked that it was a female, I was so embarrassed. Dru mentioned on the ride to the station that I should get a restraining order when she saw her following us. I filed a temporary order. I had the proof that Mae was dangerous and if it came down to it, I would fight her for my life. I'm determined not to let her have control of my life or choose who I let in it. I refuse to let her run off Taylor. I already know Dru is down for the ride with me. She made it clear she had my back. I wasn't so sure about Taylor; she needed a lot of reassurance that I was nothing like her sister. They way her round eyes squinted up at me with suspicion. I needed to show her I was strong and would fight for the both of us. I didn't want to want to fight at all but I had no choice. I wanted to wake up and believe this all was a terrible nightmare and none of this shit happened.

Dru walked out of the Detectives office with her arms around Taylor. I never thought I'd see them any less than three feet apart. Dru stared directly at me, I tried to read her face. I just saw awkwardness and that she wanted out of their embrace. I nodded at her; it was okay. Taylor needed the hug and my energy too drained to comfort anyone. We sat in the car in silence with bits of rage flowing from all of us. The police would follow up when they had more information. We had to play the waiting game while they followed up on leads, and put pieces together.

"What's next, where to now?" Dru spoke out loud to none body in particular, it sounded like she was asking herself.

"I want to get out of this city, this state. I need a vacation and my advance." I looked to Dru and her eyes were on the steering wheel like she was lost in thought.

"Sis I want to leave too; I want to go to Atlanta tonight. I have a friend named Rogue

Vanessa Robinson

waiting for me there. I just need to get some things from my place, you can give me a ride to the airport" Taylor said.

"Thank you for asking sis" even though she didn't.

"What about the investigation?"

"The police said I'm clear for now, they'll call me if they need anything else. "I'll get my mail forwarded for the test results for the HIV. I'm good I just need to get the fuck out this city. I can't breathe here knowing she's close by. If I stay here, I'll kill her, I don't care is Mae's my blood."

Her words stung. Would she kill me too, my skin crawled thinking about having to physically fight off Mae, she was supposed to be my best friend. I couldn't picture myself dragging her.

"Don't talk like that, she's our sister, she needs help" I said.

"Nobody is killing anyone!" Dru interjected. We both looked at her and she turned her head and stared out the window.

"Will you please keep in touch and let me know how you're doing?"

Her Blood

"Yeah, once I get some me time and settled in. I'll call every day. We'll catch up eventually, I still can't believe I missed out on having a good sister. Things could be so different for us."

I reached behind me in the back seat and placed my hand in hers. Taylor squeezed and held onto it until we reached her front door.

Taylor lived in a big house with more rooms than I could count and a bathroom for each one. I was surprised at how pristine the house was. Inside it looked like an interior designer had come in and put the works on it. There were marble floors in the bathrooms and all the counter tops. In spite of her beautiful house, it hurt me that she had to leave all of it behind just to escape our sister. This house was obviously her pride and joy. I followed Taylor into the back room and she was in her pulling clothes out of draws quickly folding and tossing things into her suitcase. The balcony curtains were wide open, it filled up almost the whole wall. The sky was full of orange and deep red streaks, still early in the evening; her flight wasn't until midnight. I wanted to change her mind in running away from Mae, there was nothing to be afraid of. I watched her go back and forth from the closet and bathroom, throwing things on the bed.

"Slow down girl, you're going to trip over your own two feet." I said.

"I need to get out this house, you don't know my sister —" I mean our sister, she will show the fuck up. I told her I didn't live here anymore, I put the house on the market after she started popping up asking for money."

"Funny how Mae told me she was a realtor, she even helped me find my place and did all the paperwork."

"Girl she is a professional con artist. The last time she didn't get her way she threatened my life and destroyed my property. Mae left me all kinds of voicemails of how she would kill me, I came home and all the kitchen windows were bust out. I didn't believe she would try me then but trust me I believe that bitch now. I suggest you get the fuck out of here too and let things calm down."

"I'm not running. I'm going to make sure this gets settled. Mae doesn't scare me Taylor, she's all talk."

"Oh, so you think Dru is going to protect you? What are you two supposed to be anyway? A couple? Are you fucking her?"

Her Blood

Taylor stopped folding and her head was to the side waiting for me answer. I was feeling the pressure from her to come up with some kind of explanation of our relationship.

"Yes and No. I mean yes, she would protect me but I'm a grown woman. I can protect myself. I don't know what we are but I do know she's been a wonderful friend to me."

"So, are you two fucking or not?"

"NO! and stop asking that! You're nosey as hell." The chase I was sitting on wasn't so comfortable. I wiped my forehead and my foundation was coming off on my fingers.

"Yah but you want to, you're looking hot and bothered already!!!" Taylor walked into the closet coming back with an armful of shoes and a smirk on her face.

I didn't answer her question. We made eye contact for a second and I looked away busting out in a blush.

"It's alright Sis if you want too, I know that whole thing with Mae wasn't all in your control. If you have genuine love for Dru and want to see where it goes, I won't be mad at you. I've been gay before." Taylor did a whine with her hips and a little vogue twirl, making me laugh.

"Girl we are JUST FRIENDS and I'm just dealing with too much right now, to pursue a relationship." I said.

"You don't have to convince me. I see the extra-long looks and the little touches. I think she is in love with you. Dru low key acts like she is yours already."

"Um no, I don't see that!" she was asking for too much information.

"Girl watch how she acts around you. Pay attention, don't forget that. Just be careful girl, you're in a vulnerable spot right now. Don't make any commitments, that's how you fuck up a good relationship before it even begins." Taylor dropped the pile of clothes in another suitcase and zipped it up. The suitcase looked like it was about to burst.

"Look at you trying to be all wise. I can handle this right here" I said, Waving my hand my head over my body.

"Taylor your house is dope, it looks like it cost millions to design this, please tell me how."

"Well since were bonding and all it didn't cost millions. A friend of mine Rogue in Atlanta connected me with some of her designers over here. Rogue is a good friend or whatever, she does it all. I'm going to stay with her for a few days until I find a place."

"Well dam if she is giving out free houses hook a new sister up." Taylor laughed while I gave high praise.

"It wasn't free, I used the money George left me from his will. It's a shame I have to sell it now—"... BOOM!

A loud crashing noise came from down stairs where Dru was taking a nap on the couch. Taylor and I both froze and started at each other. My heart was racing and the bile in my stomach started to burn as I stood there frozen. Taylor pointed her finger down at the stairs mouthing Dru. I shook my head at her not understanding what she was trying to say to me. Taylor tiptoed into the bathroom and I followed behind her. She slowly opened up a drawer and inside it was a black gun. Taylor grabbed the gun and we both headed to the bedroom. I motioned for her to stop and rummaged through my purse to look for the gun I had the other night. I emptied out my purse, it wasn't in there. Then I remembered Dru took it from me that night I had it pointed at my mothers' head. "FUCK"

Taylor waved her arm for me to come on and we slowly tipped toed down her stairs, barely letting our feet hit the floor. It was quiet and dark in the living room. The large flat screen was on the comedy channel playing movies earlier but now there was just a gurgling noise in the silence. I whispered Dru's name but there was no reply. Taylor was in front of me and reached behind and pinched me to be quiet. I was grabbed onto Taylors shirt because I couldn't see more than two feet in front of me. The hardwood floors were slippery underneath my toes with every step as Taylor lead me. She came to a halt and I heard her flick noise and the lights came on. I looked around the room to see what the crash noise was but nothing looked broken or fallen. Taylor and I turned around and my heart fell into my stomach. Dru was laying on the floor struggling to breath. I ran over to her sliding in the puddle of blood on the floor. There was a knife sticking out her chest and her head was bleeding profusely but she was still alive. This had to be Mae.

Taylor spinned around the room with her gun pointed every turn. "MAE YOU PSCYCHO BITCH WHERE ARE YOU?" she was screaming from the top of her lungs.

Her Blood

I had my hand on Dru's wound applying pressure, she was mouthing words but no sound was coming out.

"Don't talk baby we are going to get you to a hospital."

Mae came around the corner and stood in the dining room doorway laughing.

"So that's your boo now huh? You giving it up kind of fast Tori."

"Fuck you, delusional bitch!" I stood up from Dru and took the gun from Taylor.

"Mae you are out of your mind if you think I would ever come around you again. You don't deserve to live anymore after what you've done to us. I fucking hate you!" Mae stood there glaring at me with tears coming out of her eyes. I didn't have any empathy for her. I didn't give no fucks if she cried. She was trying to Kill everyone who loved me and the only blood I had left.

"I love you Tori, when I found out you were my sister, I didn't say anything because I was already in love with you. You were all I have, Taylor hated me since I'm not like her and momma is gone now."

Vanessa Robinson

"Don't believe shit she says Tori. She's fucking off her rocker. Mae your evil, you've been that way since you killed daddy! Yeah I know you killed him."

Mae took a step closer to me. She didn't have any weapons in her hand but I kept the gun pointed at her because she was unpredictable.

"He deserved to die, he molested me every night and momma didn't do nothing when I told her. You saw him and I let him do it to keep him off you. I know you were awake every time Taylor because you stopped snoring."

"So, what I saw. I saw you rubbing his back liking it when he was on top of you whore!"

"You knew what was happening and as my sister you didn't have my back, NOBODY did! I hate this whole family except Tori."

"You deserved it, you tortured and teased me every day of my life for being the golden child. Mae you blamed things on me that I didn't do and watched Mama beat me, snickering in my face when I cried. You earned your punishment from daddy and he never touched me bitch!!! He paid me off for your stank evil ass!!!"

Her Blood

Mae lunged full steam toward Taylor like a wild animal. Mae grabbed my arm and pulled me towards her and I pulled the trigger. The gun fired off and my hand jerked back. The blast from the gun echoed to the high ceilings. The bullet hit Mae in her shoulder and for a moment her eyes lightened up and then went dark again. I froze and Taylor grabbed the gun out of my hand. I couldn't hear anything but a high-pitched ring in my ears. I glanced over at Dru she had crawled up against the couch holding her chest. I couldn't let Mae have my family even though she was a part of it. The bullet wound didn't stop her. Mae charged again, she hoped over the glass coffee table and Taylor shot her again. Mae screamed my name and as she fell backwards onto the coffee table. Vibrations from the Glock drummed through my hand like it was attached to me. Taylor dropped it to the floor in the pile of shattered glass. I ran over to Dru and she was still alive. Taylor checked Mae's pulse and it was barely there. I knew she was dying at that very moment. A flood of relief filled me up, I could finally stop running.

~Taylor~

ATL Vibes

Atlanta was hot and humid. Unbelievable this was the same sun that shone from the sky six months ago in California. The dirty south was my new start in life. I sold the house in Cali and left behind everyone I knew there. Tori left California too and was traveling with Dru somewhere in Dominican Republic. I hadn't heard from her in a few weeks. It's been six months since I've been living with HIV. Somedays, I don't know how I'm going to make it mentally. I'm not sick, I'm just pissed off, I kill Will in my head over and over again. The police never found Laura or her son to prosecute her for his murder. I want to find her myself so I could thank her. I found out that we had another half-sister from James before he died from an overdose on heroin.

I started speaking at groups to women surviving   sexual assault and HIV prevention events. Even though I couldn't prevent my predicament it helps me see strong healthy people living with this scary disease. Talking about it makes me feel less broken and more like a whole person. I've been trying to get to in touch with Tori but she won't answer the phone. I leave her messages every other day. I thought 6 months would be along enough time for her to get over everything that transpired around Mae so we could build a friendship. That night I shot Mae I didn't feel a pulse so we left her lying on the floor. Tori dragged Dru outside to get her to the ambulance as soon as possible because she was losing so much blood. We directed them back inside to check Mae and she was gone. The cops had a manhunt for days looking for a dangerous injured woman, they came up empty handed. I called Tori again.

"Hey Sis, I promise you I was going to call you back when I had the chance, I've been preoccupied to say the least."

"Liar! I've been calling you for weeks, what's going on with you?"

"I've been in DR with Dru, she' healed now."

"What does that have to do with you not calling me back."

Vanessa Robinson

"Girl I've been busy sitting on the beach sipping margaritas, getting sand burns on my ass, perfecting this melanin."

"You don't sound like its all that. Your tone is telling me you're ready to split."

"I am ready to get out of here. My nerves are fucked up everywhere I go. Loud noises, crowds, the spatula hitting the pan to hard when Dru makes eggs in the morning. I'm suspicious of everybody. They all look like Mae. I feel like she's watching me."

"Get a gun."

"I think it's pretty clear that guns don't work on that bitch, its going to take more than that. I'm tired of watching my back. Dru ain't helping either with the eyes she has on me all the time. I feel smothered. If it's not her clocking me and hunting me down when I go the bathroom, it's her fucking security and none of them speak English."

"So, you mean to tell me that you're getting Queen of the world treatment and complaining about it! There's just no pleasing you. Are you two a thing now?"

"Damn, go ahead, jump right in all my business. We're something, its complicated. I can't trust anyone right now. I went from one person's possession to another. I'm fuckin terrified."

"I think you can trust Dru, she's just looking out for you. I was calling because I wanted you to come hang with me and O'shea. Do you know when you're coming back to the states?"

"Oh, so now your fond of Dru? I'm not buying it."

"Yeah, she almost died for you."

"Listen I'll be back soon. I don't have a date. Wait, are you drunk? you sound tipsy."

"Shit I'm something, I'm at the W hotel having a drink by my dam self since you won't come catch up with me. There's this fine ass Boris Kodjoe guy winking at me. I might be getting some tonight."

"You're fucked up! You should take a cab home. I don't think Boris wants you throw up on him."

"Tori I'm living my life here in Atlanta, nobody knows me here. Mae will never find me. I'm thinking about changing my name, finding me a husband, having my own family. I think I could be a homemaker."

"Tell me about it when you're sober. Do you tell them?"

"Tell who what?"

"That your positive. When you meet a guy, do you tell them?"

"No. why should I?"

"Well if you didn't wouldn't you be doing what Will did to you?"

"Tori that's different. He raped me. These guys out here are different, they could have something too. Its just sex. Sex is sex. If I fall in love, I'll tell him."

"Sounds dangerous sis. You shouldn't play with people like that."

"You should come here. I'm selling houses now."

"I'm proud of you Taylor."

"I have to go Boris just sent me a drink"

"Be careful."

I waved over Boris. He was slimmer than the real deal but he had those eyes. The skin on his bald head shinned. He sat on the barstool beside me grinning.

"Thank you for the drink."

"You're not from here. Women don't dress like that down here."

"Is that a compliment? Men down here don't know how to compliment a lady. Bartender do you hear this fuckery."

"Nah, I didn't mean to come off that way, you look good. You just caught me off guard. You have an amazing figure. I've never laid eyes on a woman so beautiful in Atlanta."

"Thank you. Now that's a compliment."

"What's your name?"

"Buy another round and I'll tell you."

"Just for your name?"

"That's what I said, right? Can you afford it?"

"For you, hell yeah! How about I start with me, my name is Donny nice to meet you."

Vanessa Robinson

"My name is Mae, it's a pleasure to meet you."

Her Blood

Vanessa Robinson

~O'shea~

My other sister

Here I am again, back in this nasty place. The walls looked like death was trying to come through the cracks and holes. Everything in here smelled like mildew, latex and cheap hand sanitizer. The pink chairs were so worn down, full of brown stains and rips. The woman sitting right ahead of me her whole butt and thighs were spilling over the chair like a muffin. When they bought these chairs, they didn't put into thought the real size of a woman sitting down in them.

"O'shea Grooms!" Shit they were calling me. I snatched out my head phones and headed to the front of the waiting room. The lady standing at the front said my name loudly again, eyeing the room from on top of her glasses. She stood there watching me get up with her frumpy ponytail on top her head like a scoop of ice cream about to fall off. I knew she saw me sitting there in the back with my head down listening to music. Earlier about an hour ago the lady next to me had complained my music was too loud and she signaled me from the front desk to turn it down. This is my fourth time at this abortion clinic. The first time I came in this clinic in she was nice to me, wore a sympathy smile with her lips tucked in and walked beside me. She said my name quietly when she called me up to see the doctor. On my second visit she called my name in a hushed voice, but with a question in her tone. When I walked up, she looked curious, her facial expression said "What are you doing here?" with her head tilted to the side. Now the last two times I've come in this rotten place she yells it out, like she's trying to scorn me and make a point. Old nurse knew what she was doing, whatever happen to being discreet, I should tell her boss. Then again, I just want to get this over with, I didn't need none of these people in here trying to give me a hidden lecture or judging me. As I walked up to the front everyone lifted their head when my name was called again, gawking at the girl with the bouncy afro and weird name that sounded like shea butter.

I followed the raggedy styled ponytail, flopping around her head, into the bright back area. I immediately stepped on the scale then let her take my vitals, after I sat down. I had already taken the pill the nurse gave me two hours ago. I undressed and laid on the flat bed with my legs curled up. My heart was beating fast, If I closed my eyes I could've been on a rollercoaster, scared and sick to my stomach. I was going to be awake this time. I couldn't afford anesthesia; I couldn't even afford a cab home. A nurse walked through the hall and when she passed me her eyes stayed on my stomach. It was a small round pudge fighting against the buttons on my jeans. I couldn't feel any love for what was growing inside of me. My heart was locked up in chains, unwilling to love anything including me. The machine in the corner of the room was beeping, I needed more noise to distract me from my thoughts. I should have smoked more weed, I wasn't high enough. I feared if they took my vitals and they were too elevated they would've told me to come back another day. The doctor walked in the room and stood at the end of the table I was on. I've had him before, I remember his skin pale white with a grey tinge. He embodied the color of slushy snow mixed with sod from the streets. His bright blue eyes, a light through the mud. He had a kind smile in his foreign water eyes but behind them I knew he felt sorry for me. The doctor explained the procedure to me like many times before. I nodded my head up and down and said a few "yes and sure" when he paused, as if was listening. I knew the deal. Last he asked me if "I am ready for him to perform it?" I shook my head signaling yes, "Sure Doctor" I whispered.

The machine started humming low and then got louder after it warmed up. The nurse stood on the side watching me, her eyes darting up and down my body and then back at the tube hanging out of me going into the machine. I couldn't listen to this, I couldn't see it, I should have paid for the anesthesia. The judgment in the room like a thick layer of smoke on the tip of my nose tempting to suffocate me. I put my head phones on and let Frank Ocean "God Speed" blast through my ears to my soul as tears burned my eyes.

They wheeled me out of the room and parked me in front of the sliding glass doors to wait for my ride, they would make me stay longer to make sure i was okay to walk if no one came. I told the transporter I had someone coming to pick me up but I knew I didn't have anyone coming. I wanted to get the hell out of there, the stench of the latex was made me want to throw up. I rode the bus from my house and jumped off two stops before then walked the rest of the way. I didn't want to be seen getting off the bus right in front the clinic. There were at least three other girls that did the same thing as me. The hospital staff wheeled me out to the entrance and parked me in front of the window. I sat in the wheel chair for what seemed like forever watching cars pick up and drop girls off. The staff who waited for the phantom ride with me was called inside because someone was falling out of their wheel chair. This was my chance to leave, as soon as he was out of sight, I stood up on my shaky legs and started walking home. Once I hit the end of my block I walked down to the bodega and grabbed a pint of vodka. There was no way I could sleep tonight without having a drink. I drank halfway down the bottle standing in front the store. There was a Jamaican man with bloodshot eyes sitting outside the store on a wooden ancient classroom chair. He stared hard at my ass licking his lips. Before I walked too far away, he yelled after me "Keep the problems in the bottle sexy gal, you need to smoke!" I thought about yelling back at him but I didn't have the energy. Maybe I did need a blunt or two, it might ease the pain of the ripped up feeling I had deep in my womb. I Marched right over to him and he stood up, the chair falling backwards. I handed him a twenty-dollar bill and he passed me a small bag. Walking home I could smell coming out of my purse. I knew he had some fire because he always smoking it in the morning when I was on the way to work, at least when I had a normal job.

These days the jobs I have is tricking with dates and cleaning offices here and there. No fucking benefits, vacation time, none of the shit. I can barely feed myself on those checks. I walked down past Iman park, I stopped at the corner store for something to roll with. I could feel eyes on me as I walked in the store. This African lady standing by the register stood inside everyday people watching like she was security. She stood outside the store in the evenings on her loud speaker preaching about God and saving yourself. I didn't want to hear it. I quickly turned away from her because I knew if I made eye contact, she would start up her shit and today wasn't the fucking day. A young girl, barely looking out of high school, came in behind me with three little kids following close behind her. They were begging for chips and candy and she was yelling at them to put it back. She had a baby on her hips too drooling, with big eyes staring straight at me. I couldn't help but look at him back, I stuck out my tongue and he smiled at me. His momma ordered a cigar wrap, threw a four pack of wine and the chips for the kids on the counter all with her food stamp card. If it weren't for the city clinic, I would be on my way to five kids right now, it was depressing to keep going through this.

Walking in my building, the hallways always smelled like cat piss from the strays mixed with cheap air freshener. Trash swept in corners laid out like decorations. I guess the maintenance man was on one of his special breaks. He thought he was slick, I always caught him sleeping on the stairs leading towards my apartment. I knew it was him because he snored so loud and his keys jingled when he moved. I never told his boss he was sleeping on the job because he saved my life one time. One evening a date wouldn't leave and he heard me screaming and tousling with the guy. I was nearly raped by him and he kicked my door in and fought the guy off me. He was a big guy and had muscles like he may have done a long stint in prison. His top muscles were big and his legs were small. He was old enough to be my grandfather with silver hair lined up perfectly on his face. Anytime he actually cleaned and mopped the halls, he'd say his corny line to me "Hey pretty lady, watch out old man cleaning." The cleaner would catch me coming out my door, with his head down, his eyes focusing on his mop swish back and forth. Somehow, he knew it was me without even looking up from the dirty mop. That night though he said more than he'd ever said. Once the guy ran out of my apartment, old man pointed his finger at me standing in my doorway barely catching his breath "Find you a new job pretty lady, I ain't working nights no more and I won't be able to help you next time!" He stormed out slamming my broken door, cracking the frame. I could hear the absurd number of keys bouncing off the side of his hip and his feet hobbling down the stairs. I owed him a thank you. That night I put my couch against the door for security. When I woke up the next morning out of my drunken stupor there he was kneeling in the doorway. He hammered down hard and fast into the wood, he wouldn't even look at me. I stood there trying to say thank you but I don't even know if he heard me. He acted as if nothing happened and hummed some old school tune while he fixed the door.

I was scared shitless after that and changed up my whole routine. I stopped taking random trick appointments off the street and just stuck with my regulars. I had one regular wealthy guy I knew wouldn't be going anywhere anytime soon and that was Mike. He was the only one I would leave the trade life for. Over the last two years I've been waiting for him to leave his wife. Mike promised me he would leave his bougie wife when he made enough money to pay her off. It started to feel like he was just paying me off to keep quiet about the affair. Mike spent two weekends with me a month and each time he gave me two thousand dollars for his stay. I used the money twice already to have an abortion over the last two years. Last thing I wanted for myself was to have a baby with a married man and his empty promises of a lavish future together. I didn't believe the dream he was selling me, I just wanted a little piece of it.

I never planned for my life to be like this at twenty- eight years old, but there was this guy, and I thought we fell in love. When I was twenty- one years old, I started working at bank downtown and worked my way up in two years to bank manager. I was on salary and worked long tiring hours but the money was decent, it paid the bills. My mother and step- father passed away in a car accident and I couldn't deal with them being gone. I started losing interest in everything that mattered after that. My boss Donny who always had a serious crush on me and a rumored coke habit took me under his wing. He knew I was vulnerable and one night the both of us were working late he saw me crying and invited me out for drinks. I needed to let my hair down and stop feeling sorry for myself. If I wasn't at work, I was cooped up in the house depressed because my family was gone and I was alone now. Donny was fun and everyone always spoke highly of him at work. He was six feet tall with high yellow skin, pretty teeth and good hair. Donny made sure to walk around the office in his finest winking at me leave with those sexy dimples. He would drop little sticky notes on my desk with hearts on them. I might as well go out with him since I didn't have anyone else. At the bar he was an absolute riot, we laughed, drank, danced and kicked it all night. We were having a blast and when the club started emptying out, we decided to go back to his place to continue the party.

At his high-rise apartment that overlooked the city we sat on the roof top with the music blasting. I was barefoot on a roof, in my little black dress, gazing at the stars with nothing to lose. Donny sat on the chair watching me with a smirk on his face like he had a secret. I sat down in the chair across from him that's when I saw the coke on the table. He had a small mirror with four messy lines already chopped up. He sat there with eyes squinting at me, watching to see what I would do. I pretended like it was nothing and grabbed the wine bottle gulping it down my throat. Shit, back then I wasn't much of a drinker and I was already past my two-glass limit. I was way past being tipsy. Donny pushed the plate of coke towards me "Let's let loose for real, a little bit won't hurt girl. How you think I work those longs hours and don't get tired!" He threw his hands up in the air like he won a game of spades. I stared at the plate for a minute, while Donny pranced and danced around in circles snapping his fingers. Up until that point in my life I had never done any drugs other than weed, and I barely did that. I can't remember my complete thought process then because I was so naïve. I know my job crossed my mind and I didn't want Donny to think I was some little ass girl that couldn't handle herself. I didn't want him thinking I wasn't fun or that I would be moping around the office forever. My review was coming up soon and the bank did push positive attitudes in the work environment. I put my head down to the plate and sniffed a line. My nose burned bad. I could the highest percentage bonus in the company. A down payment for a townhouse in Buckhead.

After the first line nothing happened, then I did two more. I did lines until the stars were flying straight at me. I was out of my mind I didn't sleep for almost two days, nor did I leave Donny's house. That whole weekend he fed me coke and dick. He stroked me so much my legs had those prickly stings on my skin. My pussy was swollen I could feel her when I pushed down to let the liquid flow out of me. The downward spiral of my life began that weekend with Donny.

I started doing cocaine at work with Donny and having sex with him in his office. It became an everyday thing for us, get high, fuck and work. Six months in of my drug habit I found out I was pregnant. I was four months along and didn't even notice I was almost in my second trimester. I had lost so much weight and barely ate. I figured it was impossible for me to be pregnant, somehow in my high state of mind I thought the coke was like birth control. When I told Donny was pregnant, he laughed in my face like it was joke and told me to get rid of it. He said he didn't have the money to take care of a baby and I should do what's best for both of us. I had explained to him it was too late for that and I couldn't abort the baby because I had heard his heartbeat. I had fallen in love with him already and I was afraid to tell Donny. After I told him I was keeping the baby he started treating me different at the office. Donny would nitpick at my work and make me redo long reports ad counts. Donny stopped giving me coke and I became sick. I had to find it elsewhere now and copped some from a guy on the street. After begging Donny to give me coke and threatening to expose him he ended up giving me meth in my third trimester and it was around then I stopped showing up for work. I put in for maternity leave in the ninth month of my pregnancy and stayed home and did drugs all day. I had nothing for my baby but a car seat left in front of my door by one of the neighbors. The day I gave birth to my son, I called Donny to come down to sign the birth certificate and bring me a little coke because I going through withdrawals. I thought I had hidden my drug habit well from the doctors and nurses. When I woke up from a nap, social workers were standing around my bed. They began advising me that they had been notified of my drug use by the child's father and the baby was going to be with the state now. Donny stood outside my hospital room staring at me as I cried. They advised they would test Donny at his request for a DNA test and then the case would go to family court. I had to go home without my new born baby. I was broken into pieces. I had planned to get off the drug a few months after the baby was born, but I needed more time. I was so pissed off at Donny. I went up to the bank and tried to fight him, and that's when I was fired. I was left with no pay, no baby and a nasty drug habit. I had used all of my money on drugs and had nothing to pay my rent. Donny won full custody of our son and I lost all rights to him because I no longer had a place and couldn't pass the drug test.

That year I had been arrested multiple times for possession of drugs and prostitution. Instead of the just putting me in jail, I entered in a drug rehab facility for three months and swore of drugs for good. Donny claimed he relocated to different state with our son while I was away. I haven't been able to find him or my son. Once I was able to land an apartment, one the street girls introduced me to escorting and I started taking dates to make money. Through work I met mike my boyfriend. Mike was a married man and well established, he owned two restaurants and a hotel. He had three kids with his wife but still managed to squeeze time for me. I never told Mike about my past, he just mostly talked about himself and his problems, what most johns did. Even though he was my client I cared for him, he made me feel like our world as real. When we were together it was like I was his wife and I had some type of normalcy. I wasn't just a hoe, looking for the next trick to fuck to pay her rent. Mike would fill me up at night with his dreams of us moving to Colorado somewhere and climb mountains with no worries. He would rub me down with warm oil and massage my feet and whisper to me he would take care of me forever. I knew his promises was all bullshit because he would never leave his wife. He wasn't going to lose half of his millionaire fortune to her. One evening Mike let it slip out that he didn't sign a prenup and if he filed for divorce, everything he had would be fair game for his wife. Mike's face had a puppy trapped in a cage look. I didn't care about that. As long as I was getting my part, I knew he wasn't serious and wouldn't risk all his money for me. I was getting on my feet because of the money he gave me but it still wasn't enough. I let him go bareback with me over and over because I knew if I said no, he wouldn't want me to be his mistress anymore.

Sitting on my fire escape with my legs hanging off the edge, I smoked the blunt and watched the people below move about in the streets. This area was full of poverty, drugs, and violence. At night the kids destroyed the neighborhood while their father and uncles sold drugs on the street corners. I would do anything to get out of this city and find my son. I sipped and smoked so hard I started to feel less pain in my gut. Mike was coming over in a few days and I knew he would want to play around. I had to get my nerves up to tell him that I didn't want to have sex. There would be no way I could fuck him with the heavy bleeding that I was doing. I wanted to tell him he couldn't have sex with me raw anymore. I wasn't his wife; he shouldn't even be fucking me in the first place. Hell, he should be using condoms like I asked, I couldn't get on birth control because it made me sick. I can't go back in the clinic and have another abortion. Mike owed me more money for all I had to go through to be his secret. I needed a car to move around, I had a whole millionaire coming to slums to fuck me and he was paying me barely enough to get by.

I climbed back into the window from the fire escape and laid on the bed. I checked my email but there was nothing new. I was waiting for my last check from the cleaning company. I told them I quit after they lowered the little part time hours. It didn't make sense to go a job three days a week for only two hours a day to break my back cleaning. It cost me more than they were paying me to get to the houses that they were sending me to. The jobs they had us doing were unsafe without the proper protection equipment and I was tired of begging for it. Slowly they cut my hours over a month, so I told supervisor to take his fat ass over there and clean up puddles of shit with no mask.

I was a little dizzy when I stood up, but I walked down the stairs cradling the rail to check the mail. My body was weak from the procedure and I was starting to feel the buzz. As I stood in front the mailbox jamming my key in someone walked in and stood next to me. I knew who it was without looking just by her scent. It was my neighbor Rogue. Rogue lived on the top floor in one of the loft apartments. She had deep red hair and creamy brown colored skin. I knew she had to be an escort too, that's what most of the women in this building did. Either they were selling pussy or have before and were retired from it. Each time I seen Rogue she was with a different guy or would come in with designer bags from shopping. Her place was right above mine and I could hear her walking in her heels all the time getting ready to go out. I always had an interest in who she worked for and where she pulled her tricks from. I wanted to make the kind of money she was making. She drove a Benz, that she parked right in front of the building and none of those bad ass kids ever fucked with it. They respected her on this street and she walked like she demanded. I only knew her name was Rogue because I saw an envelope sticking out the mailbox and read the name on it one day being nosey.

I turned to her and said "Hey", that was about all I could muster up with the state I was in. I dropped my mail feeling nervous that I might miss the opportunity to talk to her. She bent down to help me pick up my mail, my eyes catching her Louboutin shoes and toned sleek legs.

"Hi, ugh you don't look so good. Are you okay?"

"Yeah, I'm alright, just a little under the weather today."

I leaned onto the mailboxes to steady myself but I leaned into them too hard and the whole case rocked back. I was making a fool of myself falling all over the place. She handed me the mail began walking towards the staircase, I dragged behind her. My legs were heavy like I was carrying a tire on my head and it was slowly pushing me into the ground. I could make it up the stairs alone. I tried to hide it by stepping slow and taking wide steps each foot in front of the other.

"I can help you up the steps girl, my name is Rogue by the way" She smiled and grabbed onto my arm. She was so beautiful they way her fluffy crimson lips curled up raising her already high cheekbones.

"Thank you so much, I'm O'shea, I think I live right below you."

"Ahh you're the jazz music player, you have a great playlist. Oh, and I love the smell of your food. Are you Dominican?"

"Yeah just half, I get that from my mother and my real father is from panama I think." Mentioning my mother instantly brought a pang to my heart. Mama would be so disappointed in me if they were here to see all my fuck ups. I stopped in my tracks and we jolted forward. Rogue tried to catch my fall and dropped her bags.

"How about you come up to my place and rest a bit. I want to make sure you are okay." She had a concerned look on her face and it scared me. I may have did too much smoking and drinking in my mental state. I missed my mother, ever since they passed away my life had a timeline of pure chaos.

Rogue opened her door and it looked like we were in another building. The theme in her loft was classy and sexy, everything was in gold or white and dripping with money. This is exactly what I needed, a moment in paradise. Unlike my place the appliances were stainless steel and she had real hardwood floors. She guided me to her couch and helped me lay back with my feet up.

"I appreciate you for helping me, your place is super nice."

"No problem, I have my days too and I've seen you in the neighborhood from the window" she pointed. The window practically took up the whole wall with thick curtains to match her interior.

"If you don't mind me asking, how did you get the building to do your place like this? My place compared to yours would get demolished."

"Actually, I was one of the first ones in the building when the renovations began. Let's just say me and the contractor made a deal on the side. I actually ended up buying this space from the building owner and he's cool with any changes I make."

"Girl you hit the jackpot! You own the building?"

"No just this condo, they didn't make you an offer too?"

"No, I drop my check in the mail, I've never met the owner, everything is through text or email."

Rogue handed me a mug with steaming tea and I sipped it slow.

"This is good, what is it?" I never had tea that tasted so good.

"It's earl grey" she sat in front of me on the ottoman smiling watching me drink it. I started to feel sleepy and my eyes were getting heavy. I definitely drank too much today for my body. Rogue took the mug from my hand. I laid my head back staring up at her high ceilings wishing my place was as serene as it was in here. It smelled like home in here.

I could hear my son calling me, he kept repeating "Mommy, mommy wake up. I'm right here mommy." I turned my head and, on my shoulder, there was a small chocolate boys hand shaking me clasped onto my shirt. When I opened my eyes to see my sons face finally there was Rogue was standing over me with her hand on my shoulder trying to wake me. Damn. Another one of those dreams, I could never see my sons face in the dreams. After giving birth to him, I held him for an hour before they took my baby away from me permanently. I was too worried about getting high in the hospital, I didn't take the time to study his features or make sure he had all his fingers and toes. I never did say goodbye. My baby always came to me in my dreams.

"Are you still in the fog?" Rogue asked, she was dressed in different now. She wore a tight money green cocktails dress. It hugged all her curves and it screamed "pay me."

"I'm okay, just was having a silly dream. That tea you gave me knocked me out, can I use your bathroom before I head out?" she looked hesitant at first but shook her head up and down. After I used the bathroom, while washing my hands I opened the medicine cabinet. My mother always told me you can tell a lot about a person by the medicine their prescribed. There were three bottles of Motrin in the cabinet next to some expensive face cream and anxiety medication. There was an absurd number of condoms underneath the sink. A small pink metal box was hidden under a bag of cotton balls, I tried to open it but it was locked. I placed it back gently where I found it. I checked myself to make sure I didn't look crazy. My hair was all over my head from passing out. I used Rogues brush to bring my afro back to life. My presentation was everything to me and today I didn't look like I just didn't give a fuck.

Rogue was sitting at her bar sipping out of a champagne glass. She looked like a model, everything about her was on point. Rogue didn't look like she missed a coin that came her way.

"Can I ask what do you do for a living?" I sat on the bar stool next to her.

"Honey I do the same thing as you, chase the fucking bag!" she chuckled a little bit and began pouring me a drink.

"I mean I have a few regulars but I don't think I make as much money as you, I want more—" I didn't want to say too much about my past and my son just yet, I didn't know her like that.

Vanessa Robinson

"Well how about this, I can introduce you to my boss this weekend they are having a gathering with some clients. Would you like to be my date?"

"Yeah, but I don't have anything to wear to something like that."

"You can borrow something of mine. Like I said I've seen you around and your wardrobe is super chill. No shade. How does Thursday night sound?"

"I'll be there."

"My friend is coming, I can't wait for you to meet her, she says she knows you.

"How when I just met you?"

"I'll let her tell you."

"I'm feeling set up right now."

"No don't, I promise you it's nothing bad. I think you two may have a relative. She mentioned your name and I just put it together."

"Who is it?"

"Your real father."

"I never met my real father, how do you know all this? This is a little too creepy for me."

"Look here's her number, call her."

Rogue handed me a phone number written on a piece of paper. I told her I would see her tomorrow to go shopping. I sat on the couch and dialed the number. Who was this girl that knew all my business?

TO BE CONTINUED..............................